THE SECOND WIFE

NJ MOSS

www.bloodhoundbooks.com

Print ISBN: 978-1-5040-8011-8

For my wife, Krystle x

1

SCOTT

S cott pushed open his front door with a smile. It was his and
Casey's first-year anniversary, and he was glad to be home
from school. One of his students had been difficult, taking out
her phone repeatedly, causing a scene when he confiscated it.
Scott loved his work: inspiring the kids' passion for history, the
sense of fulfilment when a student told him they wanted to
study it at college, the knowledge he was having a positive effect
on the world.

But there was no denying children could be very, very
annoying.

These were problems for Monday. He had the whole
weekend to spend with his wife. His *second* wife. When Scott
thought about what had happened to his first, Natalie, his chest
got tight. He wondered if that would ever go away. The guilt
didn't help.

Natalie had killed herself in the garage; Scott had found
her. He'd never forget how she'd looked sitting there. He didn't
let himself think about it often. And then, seven months after
her death, he and Casey had met at a bar and bonded straight
away.

People said seven months was too fast to move on. They were even more outraged when he and Casey married a month later. It didn't help that Casey and Natalie had been in the same book club, a fact Scott only learned two weeks into seeing her... and by then, it was too late. He was already obsessed.

Casey had been exactly what he needed. She was compassionate, attentive. They were always making each other laugh. She'd rescued him from the darkness of his grief. Scott didn't care what people said. He and Casey were happy.

"Hello?" he called.

Casey had sent him a text that afternoon.

I've got a surprise for you later xxx

Scott's mind filled with all the possible meanings. Casey's surprises often involved mad adventures in the bedroom. That was another thing that had bonded them so quickly: the world-shattering sex.

"I'm in here," Casey called from the living room.

Scott walked in to find her sitting on the armchair, her legs crossed, a glass of wine in her hand. He'd expected her to be wearing the lingerie he'd bought her the previous week, but she was in her favourite pyjamas, with a hole in the T-shirt.

Even so, she was beautiful. Her red hair spilled down to her shoulders. Without make-up, her features were soft and almost elfish. Scott felt intoxicated every time he looked at her.

"Take a seat."

"You're making this sound like a job interview."

"Take a seat, Scott."

He did as she said, wondering why she was speaking so strangely. Her tone was low. Her eyes had a quality he'd never seen before; normally they were open, caring, but now they had a nasty glint.

2

"Is something wrong?" he asked.

She finished her wine and slammed the glass on the coffee table. She didn't use a coaster, which was as unusual as the change in her demeanour. "Just our whole marriage really."

"What? I don't–"

"Shut up."

Scott sat back, as though she'd physically struck him. "Is this some sort of joke? Happy anniversary, by the way."

"There's nothing happy about it. In fact, there's been nothing happy about this entire marriage. The whole thing has been a charade. The whole thing has been leading up to this moment. And finally – *finally* – I don't have to pretend anymore."

Scott stared down at the pinkie finger of his left hand, cut away at the second knuckle from an injury he'd received in university. He looked at his wedding band, silver this time; it had been gold with Natalie. He faced Casey again, struggling to think of a response.

"I need you to be quiet while I explain a few things," she said. "Do you think you can manage that?"

She never spoke to him like this. Even if he was being grumpy after a hard day at school, she was always patient and understanding.

"I asked you a question," she snapped.

"Explain what?"

"Open your emails. I've sent you something."

Scott took out his phone and tapped the relevant icon. Casey's message had no subject, no text, just an attached video. He clicked it; the video downloaded and then started to play.

The first minute was a slideshow of photos: all of which had clearly been taken in secret. Scott was asleep in bed, naked. He was standing in the shower, mouth open in mid-conversation. She must've been pretending to use her phone, discreetly snapping shots. There were photos of him sitting on the toilet. More of him naked in bed.

Other videos played.

She must've hidden the camera in the corner of the bedroom, near the dresser drawers. The angle had been expertly chosen. He and Casey were having sex, but Scott could only see his own face, his own shifting body. Casey was on the bottom, out of view. The video changed, and now he was standing at the edge of the bed – Casey still out of view – masturbating.

Scott tossed his phone onto the sofa cushions.

"There are more," Casey said. "But this gives you an idea."

"I don't understand."

"It's simple." She smiled in a way he'd never seen before, all teeth. "I've been pretending this whole time. I never loved you. I was thinking about other people every time we had sex. I think you're a pathetic and selfish man."

Scott blinked. There were tears in his eyes. He pawed angrily at his face as he leapt to his feet. "Casey, what is this? What are you playing at?"

"Would you agree that your career as a secondary school teacher would be ruined if these videos found their way into the wrong hands?"

Scott loomed over her. He'd never hit a woman, but his body was taut. He wanted to snap, to shout, to flip the coffee table.

"Honey, please." Casey sighed. "You can stand there trying to look tough all you want, but it doesn't change anything. Answer my question."

"Yes. Obviously it would have an effect on my career."

"So you agree you don't want me to release these videos?"

Scott felt like he was hallucinating. He leaned down, meaning to place his hand on her shoulder; then she would smile for him in that just-Casey way, so sweet, so affectionate, and tell him she'd never hurt him.

She stared coldly. "Sit down. I don't want you anywhere near me."

"Casey–"

"Sit down or I send the videos to every member of staff at your school. Now, Scott."

Scott returned to the sofa. "Why are you doing this?"

"As if I'd tell you that." She giggled; just like with the weird smiling, he'd never heard her laugh like that before. "I didn't plan on making it last a full year. I had everything I needed after a couple of months. But the thought, it was too captivating, too interesting. Our first-year anniversary. Just look at your face. That alone was worth it. Are you *crying*, you big baby?"

Scott rubbed his cheeks again, coughing back tears. He'd not always been so quick to cry, but something had happened during his twenties. He'd drowned himself at Natalie's funeral.

He needed to wake up; this couldn't be happening.

"I haven't told you the best bit yet," Casey went on. "I've set up an email list with all the staff in your school on it, like I mentioned. But I've also put Natalie's parents on there, a few local newspapers, some online clickbait websites that would eat this up. With a single press of a button – *poof*, your life will never be the same again."

The previous night they'd held each other into the early hours, talking softly about how happy they were, how well their marriage was going. She'd told him she couldn't imagine being with anybody else. She'd even teared up a little, as they clung tighter and tighter.

Where had that woman gone? Had she ever been real?

"I've set up a draft, so the email will automatically send in twenty-four hours. If anything happens to me, the email will send. Every twenty-four hours I'll reset the timer."

Scott imagined the head teacher's expression as she received the email, the way it would drop, the way her eyebrows would knit and her hand would tremble on the computer mouse. He saw parents looking at him with disgusted glances, and he heard the kids jeering as he left school.

"Aren't you going to say anything?" Casey beamed.

"Can you please just explain why? We can talk about this. We don't have to–"

"Give me your phone."

"Why?"

"Because if you don't, I'll send the emails right now."

She took her phone from the arm of the chair, typed in her passcode, and stared at him. "Don't test my patience. I've had enough of that for the past year. God, you're so slow and boring and annoying and... your phone, *now*."

Scott found himself doing as she said. The threat of the videos – and the inevitable end of his career – was too high.

She took it and began tapping away.

"What are you doing?" he asked.

"I've cropped your dick in one of the photos. I'm going to send it to Lauren so you know I'm serious."

He bolted to his feet. Lauren was the teaching assistant who often worked in his class. They'd never had an intimate moment.

"You can't do that."

Casey shrugged as she threw his phone at him. "I already have."

The phone struck him in the chest, slamming like his heartbeat.

He picked it up off the floor.

She was telling the truth. In their text thread – which they used to discuss strictly school-related matters – there was a photo of his penis. And, worse, the status of the message immediately changed from *delivered* to *read*.

A moment later, Lauren's name flashed up on the screen. She was ringing him.

Casey tittered. "That was quick. I'd answer if I was you. Oh, and put it on speaker. I want to hear everything. Let's see if you can squirm your way out of this one."

2

CASEY

This was too good. Scott looked shell-shocked. It was so much better than Casey had dreamed. And the way his voice trembled as he answered the phone, that was the cherry on top.

A year she'd waited, biding her time, knowing it would hit him so much harder if it came on their wedding anniversary. Plus, Scott was useful. He had money. He had a nice house. He had all the things Casey deserved, but she was done pretending to be harmless and pathetic.

"Lauren?"

"Why did you send me this?" Lauren said.

"I... it was a mistake."

Casey drunk in every inch of him, her husband, the pathetic waste of skin to whom she'd tethered herself for reasons she wouldn't share with him. Her body was pulsing, sparkling. She felt more alive than she had in a year. She felt like *herself*; pretending was easier for her than most people, but it was still a chore. She was relieved to be back.

"A mistake?" Lauren said after a pause.

His eyes flitted to Casey, oh-so cautious. He wasn't a bad-looking man. He was tall and lean and had cutting features. His eyes were a nice shade of blue. But Casey felt nothing for him. Or, rather, she was *beginning* to feel something, though he wouldn't like it.

"Scott? You need to talk to me. You can't send me stuff like that."

"I meant to send it to Casey." He groaned. "I swear. I'm so sorry. I don't know what I was thinking. I opened my texts and clicked your name by accident. I'd never send you something like that."

"Squirm, squirm, squirm," Casey whispered.

"Are you sure?" Lauren said. "Because if you're confused about what we are, what our relationship is, I mean... I'll have to leave the school. Or you will. I've got a partner."

"I know, I know." He spoke quickly, sounding like he might start blubbing again. "I promise. I don't feel that way about you. I'm so embarrassed. Can you please delete the photo and we'll pretend this never happened?"

"Imagine if you'd sent that to one of the other teachers by mistake. Imagine if you'd sent it to the head."

"Lauren, please."

She sighed down the phone. Casey almost wanted to speak up, to thank Lauren for making Scott's cheeks turn so deliciously pale. "Let's put it behind us. But if anything like this ever happens again—"

"It won't."

"If it does, I'll have to do something."

"I understand. I feel like such a moron. I'll be more careful in the future."

"I hope so. Let's not mention this on Monday. Let's never mention it again. Sound good?"

Scott nodded like an overeager dog. "Yes."

"See you Monday."

"Bye."

Scott slumped on the sofa, letting his head fall back as he stared up at the ceiling. Casey savoured every moment, every hitch in his breath. She imagined she could smell his terror in the air, a scent like sweat. Her body was thrumming with the magnitude of it all; for the first time in over a year, she felt genuinely excited.

"What are you thinking about, honey?"

He returned his gaze to her, staring bleakly. "That could've ruined my whole damn life. It still could. One tweet about what just happened, one conversation with the head, one Facebook post, and I'm done. I'm over."

"It sounds like you're finally getting the point."

He rubbed his hands up and down his face, then through his hair, and finally he sat forwards. "What do you want?"

"I've already got what I want. You on a hook, wriggling, trying to get free. But there's no more *free*, not for you. Now be a dear and transfer me three thousand pounds."

"What?"

"I didn't stutter."

She was tempted to start the entertainment early, though she'd planned to ease him into it, break him down little by little. His tone was unacceptable; his tone was – and she hated this cliché in herself, but it was no less true – her father's voice.

"You've got seventy-two thousand in savings," she went on, burying that hateful thought. "The remainder of what you inherited from your dear dead daddy; you've been quite a flagrant spender, sweet Scottie; cruises with Natalie, renovations for the house, play-acting the rich boy. And, of course, there's the nasty business of your mother still being alive. Your stupid father left that swollen pig quite the sum, right?"

"Casey..."

"But it's still a decent amount," she cut in smoothly. "I would like three thousand. It's not an unreasonable request."

"No."

Casey laughed. It started quiet, something like the laughter she'd affected when she was the make-believe Casey, the implausible wife who was always horny and always eager to clean the house and never had a word of complaint. She was a fantasy, and Scott had fallen for her; it wasn't her fault he was so gullible. But then the laughter morphed, until she was gasping, tears rising in her eyes.

It was a release like a transformation; she was becoming a werewolf. She was growing into her real skin, not this fakeness. She wasn't the woman who woke up early just to make *her man* breakfast. She wasn't the bitch who stood there, silent, not even caring about her own kids, all to please the big bad man of the house.

It was pathetic. They were: men.

"No?" She picked up her phone. "You might want to reconsider, Scottie."

He grinded his teeth from side to side, just one of his countless annoying habits. "Casey–"

"You're not getting the point. You can give me all the puppy-dog eyes you want, but it won't change anything. Send the money. Don't make me end this before it gets good."

"Why do you need three grand?"

"If you speak again before you've sent the money, I release everything I have. Dick pics and fuck vids and all the rest of it."

More teeth grinding; more staring. He wanted to hit her, to hurt her. Which was hardly a surprise. "You're not even my wife."

"You're an idiot. Don't make me do it."

"Who are you?"

Casey stared, her thumb poised over her touchscreen. He'd

called her bluff, which was bloody annoying. But she'd get her way. She'd wear him down. There was something: a feeling.

Finally, he picked up his phone and started tapping. After a minute or so, the notification appeared: three thousand pounds, just like that, the easiest money she'd ever made. It was time she started taking care of her needs, her desires, instead of pandering to her husband all the time.

What sort of life was it, living as the woman her husband wanted her to be, a projection, not even real? In his eyes, she was a robot, a meal-prep sexbot android with no thoughts or desires of her own.

"I loved you," Scott said. "I *love* you."

"You don't even know me. But I know you. And I've never loved you. I wouldn't be able to. I think it's your bedtime, honey. I've got some shopping to do."

Scott glanced at the window, at the autumn sunlight slanting through the glass. "My *bedtime*?"

"Yes. Stay upstairs for the rest of the night. I can't stand to look at you any longer."

He tried to appear tough again, but it didn't matter. She could see right to the core of him. She'd lived with him since before they were married; she'd been there during the night terrors, waking in a scream, sheets soaked in sweat, tragic ranting as he vomited up all his secrets and his pain at Natalie's suicide. There was nothing left in Scott. If there had ever been a man there, it was dead now. He was exactly what she needed him to be.

As she predicted, he obeyed. Rising to his feet, he skulked from the room like the coward he was.

Casey picked up her phone and went to the clothes website she'd been browsing a few days earlier. She felt a spree coming on.

3

SCOTT

Scott stood at the window, looking down on the street. A few kids were kicking a football at the opposite end. The sun hadn't even set.

She'd *sent him to bed*. He tried to wake up: to stop dreaming. This couldn't be happening. Casey loved him. They were happy. They had never even had a proper argument, or even a disagreement. It had been perfect.

Maybe it had been *too* perfect.

He paced up and down the bedroom. Casey's bedside table had her latest thriller on it; his had a chunky book on Winston Churchill. Her hair straighteners and her hair dryer and her make-up sat on her vanity unit. A set of lacy underwear was on the floor, near a sock. It all looked so offensively normal.

He couldn't fit it into his head; his whole life had changed. He wondered how a man would react to this, which was a stupid thing to think; he was one, or he was supposed to be. He'd *been* more of a man in university, before marriage, before life, before Natalie. But he couldn't summon that fire anymore. He blinked; tears were in his eyes.

Remembering the conversation with Lauren, he dropped

onto the bed. He'd never sent an inappropriate text, made a pass at a colleague, anything. Casey had said she wanted him to know she was serious. There was no mistaking it. This wasn't a joke. This was a trap. This was a goddamn ambush.

He lay down and stared at the ceiling.

———

That weekend, Scott lived in a fever dream. Casey treated him like her personal servant, sending him into the kitchen to collect drinks and snacks as she reclined on the sofa and watched reality TV. If he didn't arrive quickly enough, she'd ring a bell. A *bell*.

Scott thought he was imagining it the first time.

But no. There she was, the woman of his dreams, tinkling a bell he couldn't remember seeing before. She must've bought it especially for this occasion.

"There's a good boy," she said, as he put down a tray laden with biscuits and lemonade. She grinned up at him. "Oh, and by the way, I've quit my job. I don't feel like working anymore. That's okay, isn't it, honey? You'll support me."

Scott searched her face, but any sign of his wife had vanished. There was nothing. Perhaps this was Casey's identical twin. She'd returned and slaughtered the real Casey, and now she was determined to ruin her life. Was that possible? It sounded ridiculous. And yet this whole thing was so absurd, he wasn't going to dismiss anything without evidence.

"Scott, I asked you a question."

He tried to make himself snap at her, tell her it wasn't okay, the demeaning way she was speaking to him. It was the video, her blackmail, but it was the expectant look on her face too.

"Yes." The video played on a reel in his mind, distorted

14

naked writhing, and his face, twisted in pleasure. "I'll support you."

"How lovely. Anyway, off you pop. I'll ring if I need you." He eyed her phone, resting on the arm of the chair. She tittered. "Silly boy. I change my password daily, the same time I update the email draft. But go on, give it your best try. If you fail, however, my sweet slow husband, you know what happens…"

Scott left the room. Yeah, he knew what would happen. She'd wreck his life: *their* life. Except there was no *them* anymore. There never had been.

She wasn't even talking the same. She was normally soft-spoken, straightforward. But now it was like she was playing some part. Like she was trying to be this insanely theatrical melodramatic actor. He read alternate history novels sometimes, *what ifs*, and maybe that was it. He'd woken up in the wrong life.

But no. Scott didn't have that luxury. His wife was…

She'd planned this with the skill of a *psychopath*. That was it: what she was. That was where the evidence was pointing.

The email draft meant he couldn't do anything. Even if she was arrested, he wouldn't be able to access her account and delete the email. If he hurt her physically – which he wouldn't – the email would send.

Except, there was one thing. He could find out why she was doing this.

On the Sunday afternoon – after a day and a half of playing butler – he approached her cautiously. She was wearing her nightie, her bare legs crossed, the fabric open in a slit to show a glimpse of her chest. Scott fought his instincts, as his body told him to go to her, to hold her, to be with her.

"Casey." He felt like a kid in one of his classes, asking to go to the toilet. "I was wondering if I could go to the pub with Gary. I won't be long."

It felt so natural, asking her permission. Too natural. It shouldn't be that way. He was tightening the collar around his own throat, but he didn't know how else to behave around her. Not anymore. He'd thought he found a caring gentle person, but she was cutting him, just by staring. In the way she smiled.

Widely, she grinned a moment longer before speaking. "Why?"

"Because he's my friend. Because we arranged to go. He might get suspicious if I cancel."

"Hardly. People cancel all the time. Tell him you're busy raping one of your students."

Scott stared at her. She spoke so casually. And worse still was the visceral reality of her words, as though she'd forced the image into his head. He'd rather die, rather kill than even think about doing that. Such a sick thing had never even occurred to him; she was bluntly invading his mind.

Even now, he wondered. This wasn't how Casey talked.

But she was gone. Casey would never say that, not his wife.

Giggling, she waved a hand. "Don't be so serious. It was only a joke."

"Please."

"Are you begging?"

He wanted to tell her no, but his tone had become wheedling. He hated it. "I just want to–"

"Beg, and I'll let you go." She sat up, her dressing gown falling aside to reveal one of her breasts. Scott's body betrayed him, as though it hadn't yet learned what his mind knew. She laughed and pulled the dressing gown down completely, her other breast spilling free. "You're a sick bastard, you know that? You still want me *now*?"

"No," he snapped.

"So, are you going to beg?"

"Please–"

"Beg or you'll never see Gary again. I'll make sure of it. On your knees. Chop-chop."

Scott needed to see his best friend. Not only did he want to talk to somebody – Gary had always been there for him – but he simply couldn't stay here. Every time he brought her a drink, every time she threw a casual cruel comment at him, he felt little pieces of himself being chipped away.

He tried not to think about what he was doing as he lowered himself to his knees. "Please, Casey."

"More," she whispered.

"Please let me go to the pub."

"Again."

"Please let me see my friend."

She touched his face, forced him to look at her. She'd never looked so happy, not even on their wedding day, not even when he'd proposed in a whirlwind of romance and lust and primal hunger. "Yes, you sad little nobody, you can go and see your dull friend. But don't forget who's in charge. Don't forget what happens if you betray me."

If he betrayed *her*.

"I won't," he lied. "I promise."

4

SCOTT

"You all right?" Gary placed the pints down and took his seat. "No offence, but you look like a turd."

Scott tried to smile at his friend, but it felt wrong. They'd been meeting for a Sunday evening pint for years, a tradition that had started soon after their university days. Normally they'd talk about work or memories or rugby or their families, but Scott had hardly been able to say more than a hello since he'd arrived.

"Mate?" Gary was the same age as Scott – thirty-six – but taller and bulkier. His hair was a cropped afro, and freckles scattered across his cheeks. "You're acting like a weirdo. What is it?"

"It's..." Scott picked up his pint, took a sip, made the sip longer. By the time he placed it down, there was less than half left. The alcohol rushed around his body, welcome, numbing him a little. But not enough.

"Anniversary didn't go well?"

Scott laughed gruffly. He only realised how loud he'd been when a family of four looked up from the adjacent table. The pub was bustling. "You could say that," he said, lowering his voice.

Gary looked at Scott's hand: at the missing pinkie finger specifically. He was always doing that. "It can't be that bad. You and Casey have an argument or something?"

"An argument," Scott repeated. "I don't know if that does it justice."

"Don't keep me in suspense."

"I'm not sure you're going to believe me."

"Try me."

Scott told him. It all came out in a rush, beginning with returning home and ending with him on his knees, begging to be able to come to the pub. He wouldn't have told anybody else that part, but he saw Gary as the brother he'd never had. They shared everything; Scott remembered the way Gary had screamed, the blood, the agony and the fear. He'd never forget the bond they'd forged that night in uni.

"This is a joke." Gary narrowed his eyes. "No? Not a joke?"

"Nope."

"Jesus Christ."

"Yep."

Scott had known Gary long enough to tell when he wanted to say something. And, in this case, Scott didn't have to guess what.

"Go on." He sighed. "We both know where this is heading."

Gary raised his hands. "No idea what you're talking about."

"You told me so. You warned me. It was too fast. I shouldn't marry somebody who was friends with Nat. If I had to, I should've waited. Casey's too good to be true. No woman wants to have sex all the time, clean all the time, watch all my favourite films all the time. I'm an idiot. I married a stranger. I deserve this."

"Easy. I wouldn't go that far. But yeah, there's some truth in that. Something smelled off. I thought she was after your dad's money."

"She is."

"But it's not just that, is it?" Gary said. "If it was, she would've done this a long time ago. She wouldn't have waited a year."

"She said she had everything she needed after a couple of months, but it was too... what was it? Captivating, interesting. How messed up is that?"

"She sounds like a psychopath."

"She probably is," Scott whispered, his eyes getting glassy. A shiver moved over his ribs, making them feel fragile, like they could crack any moment. He imagined Casey's heel; but surely it wouldn't go *there*. "I can't believe I let this happen."

"All right, that's enough. Neck that and then we'll get another drink and figure out what we're going to do."

Scott drank the rest of his beer and slammed the glass down. When he made to stand, Gary shook his head and stood. "It's my round," Scott said.

"I reckon these are special circumstances."

Gary walked across the bar, limping a little on his left side. It had been years, but Scott still felt like hitting somebody when he thought about what had happened. Mostly, he wanted to hit himself now; punch himself so hard he jolted back into the person he'd been.

Leaning against the bar, Gary was probably taking weight off his aching leg. He'd been in the rugby team once; he'd talked often about running marathons. In the winter, if his leg was feeling particularly bad, he used a walking stick.

Scott waited, then Gary returned, placing the beers down. "So we can assume this is personal in some way. It's not just for the money."

"I think that's a fair assumption."

"The question is why, then. Why is she doing this?"

"She wouldn't tell me."

"What a surprise." Gary tapped his fingernails against the table. "We need to find out as much about Casey as we can. If she's doing this now, I'd wager she's done stuff like this before."

Scott sighed. "You a policeman now?"

"Don't huff at me. Aissa's addicted to crime docs. She even falls asleep to them. I've picked up a thing or two. And accountants have to be investigators from time to time, believe me. Where can we start?"

"I don't know. The truth is – and I know, I'm an idiot, I'm a moron, you were right – but the truth is I don't know a single thing about my wife. I've never met her parents. She's told me hardly anything about her childhood. I don't know any of her friends. I just, I don't know, I accepted her for what she is, was, was pretending to be."

Scott had held her when she cried one evening, whispering into his chest that she wanted to start fresh; he wanted this Casey, the perfect woman he loved, to be the only one he ever thought of. He'd inferred it was something bad with her parents, but there was nothing else; he'd accepted everything she'd done for him like the reflex of breathing after emerging from water.

"She preyed on you. You were still grieving. Stop beating yourself up."

"She knew Natalie, from the book club. Maybe I could start there. This could have something to do with her suicide. Revenge on her old book-club pal, maybe."

"It's a lead."

"A lead." Scott took a large sip of beer. "Three days ago I was happy. Now I'm talking about leads."

"I know. But we'll sort this."

"You know what people said, after Nat..." He saw her flesh, her pale flesh, and he was on his knees, weeping, begging; his heart was pounding up his neck and choking him, and he just wanted her to be okay. Despite all that had happened between them; despite all that could never be shared. He shook his head, dispelling the memories. "When a wife dies, even if it's a suicide, people blame the husband."

"Not always."

"But sometimes," Scott said firmly, thinking of a couple of people in particular. "Maybe Casey thinks I had something to do with Natalie's death."

"All the more reason to find a way to get her to back off," Gary said. "The idea you had anything to do with it... it's ridiculous."

"It's just an idea. Maybe her motive is something else. Maybe it's just money."

"Either way, we need to find out."

Scott nodded. "There's something else. I probably should've told you this a long time ago. Natalie left a note."

"What?"

"Yeah. It made no sense. *Down by the hangman's broken tree, we carved our names, and I hope that's where I'm going now.* I planned on trying to find out what she meant, once I'd stopped grieving, if it ever stops. But then Casey came into my life and I forgot about everything except her. I wanted to put the past behind me."

The last part was true, wanting to put the past behind him. The rest, forgetting it, was a lie; he'd never forget that note, the sinking feeling in his gut as he read it, as though all the pain and growth and arguments and setbacks and love and hate had meant nothing. There was somebody else. But he wanted it all to die, the relationship with his first wife. Everything to crumble away.

"I thought I'd reinvented myself," he muttered, feeling the alcohol hit him.

"What does it mean?" Gary asked. "The note."

"I have no idea. But it's time I found out. I still don't know why she did it, why she took her own... we were happy, I think. I hope we were." Scott's head swam, and he realised he was going to have to get a taxi home; he also knew his friend could never know the depths of his relationship with Nat. "If Casey's doing this because of Natalie's suicide, solving the note might help."

"What is it again?" Gary asked. Scott repeated it, and Gary typed it into his phone. "I have to say it, just so it's been said."

"What?"

"You should go to the police. What she's doing is illegal."

"I know. But she'll release the videos and the photos. Then I'm screwed."

"Yeah. I don't think you should go either. But I had to say it."

They drank quietly for a while, listening to the pub sounds, the fruit machine and the clinking of glasses and the laughter and the life going on around them. Scott felt disconnected from it all, similar to the way he'd felt after Natalie's passing, and for long periods before, as though he was inside a bubble.

If he'd learned one thing after Natalie, it was that life went on, always, no matter what. There was only one thing which ended it. Which meant he either had to die or fight, and he wasn't going to give up.

He tried to convince himself of these words, but then he felt a tremor, like a blow to the chin. Fighting his own wife, the woman he loved, the woman he'd thought he was going to spend the rest of his life with.

This was no longer a marriage. It was war.

He finished the dregs of his pint.

5

CASEY

Casey whistled a tune as she pulled out the drawers and upended their contents. The mess of their life spilled out over the living-room floor: notebooks and knick-knacks and a small teddy bear Scott had won at the arcade during one of their earlier dates. She'd hugged him so tightly, shifting her body against his, and then he'd started to whinge about how special this was, how much it meant to him.

"I know it doesn't seem very manly, getting all emotional over a teddy."

Casey had whispered it was okay. He didn't have to be ashamed. And all the while she was singing within. "This is just the beginning, sweet husband-to-be," she wanted to tell him. "It's all downhill from here."

"It's so good to feel again," he'd croaked, smearing his lips across her forehead in what was intended to be a romantic way; at least Casey assumed that's what he was going for. He failed. "I know it's silly."

"No," she'd lied. "I understand. You've been through a lot. I'm just so glad I can be here for you."

Scott had no right, imposing his mood on her, which he did

incessantly. If she ever found an equilibrium – a reprieve from the devil in her thoughts – his whining or loving or self-pitying or wannabe man tone would come leaking in. *I thought it'd be nice if we watched a film tonight...*

And Casey, acting like a professional, with more commitment than most people could even contemplate. *Oh, you pick, Scott. You always pick the best films.*

Then his grin, self-satisfied when she reflected his own naïve aspirations back at him. He was always on the edge, Scott, limp. Wet. A soaked sort of man.

She hummed a tune as she tipped over the coffee table. Her back ached as she dragged the armchair onto its side, and then she threw the cushions across the room. She'd already handled the rest of the house. The bedroom was a bomb site. The kitchen was covered in mess, the Aga drenched with curry and pasta and casserole sauces, the glass jars shattered on the floor. The bathroom was streaked in shower gel and shampoo.

With her work done, she sat on the sofa, the one piece of furniture she'd spared.

Scott was going to pretend he didn't deserve this. He'd already started, asking her why she was doing this. He was acting like he didn't know. But he did, and really it made no difference if he admitted it or not.

A small voice whispered from deep inside, telling her he *couldn't* admit it. But she ignored it. It was wrong. She'd seen it herself. She'd taken care of the complications. Casey was an expert at walling off certain parts of her mind and letting others flourish; she'd survived more than most people could imagine. That was why almost everybody was just terrible to be around: the assumption they deserved to be unbroken.

This mental control was what made her so much cleverer than everybody else; it was what made life so fun.

She rose when the front door opened, walking into the

hallway. Scott paused. He looked at the shattered mirror that lay directly beneath him, at the ornaments scattered everywhere. "What happened?"

"I trashed the place. You're going to have it spotless by the time I get home."

"Why?"

"You and your *whys*. You're missing the point. I don't have to explain anything to you."

He stared, trying so desperately to appear innocent. But there was no such thing as innocence. It was just a word to describe something which existed only in people's minds. Or, if it was real, it was only there so somebody could take it. That was all. There was no in-between.

Scott looked like he might cry again. He wasn't a manly man at all.

"Where are you going?" he asked.

She was going to pick up some weed and have a smoke as she walked along the Bristol waterfront, but she wouldn't tell him that. He didn't even know she smoked. Let him imagine she was out plotting more schemes, more ways to hurt him. Like he'd hurt others – and the rest, the disconnect, the issues, the obstacles? Casey used her magic trick; she walled it away. No need to think about it.

His shoes crunched over the broken glass. He paused inches from her. He reeked of booze. "Is the rest of the house like this?"

"It's worse."

"It's going to take hours. I've got school in the morning."

"How is that my problem?"

He tried to glare, but he looked more like a pouting child. "This is so bloody immature."

"I don't care."

"But *why*?"

Casey waved her hand, coming close to his face, just about

26

missing. She hadn't struck him yet. "Because I can. Because I want to. Because I'm in charge. You're so slow and boring and, *urgh*, just get out of my way."

He didn't move.

Casey smirked. "Are you going to hit me, big man? I bet you want to. I bet it's all you can think about. The sound your fist would make as it crushes against my cheek. The feel of your knuckle cracking against my face. I bet it makes you hard, doesn't it?"

He stepped aside. "Something's wrong with you."

"I could make you eat glass for saying that. You need to be more careful."

Casey left the house and strolled down the street, whistling as the cool evening air pleasantly caressed her cheeks. An elderly lady came walking up from the opposite direction, one of those crones who stare at anybody and everybody with their talk-to-me eyes. Casey couldn't imagine being so pathetically reliant on a few words of conversation here and there.

"What's got you so chipper, dearie?" the lady called.

"The impossible has happened." Casey beamed as she came to a stop. It was easy; it helped that she'd been acting, in a sense, ever since she was seven years old. "My husband has offered to clean the house. Can you believe it?"

The lady chuckled. "That is quite the event. Let's hope he does a good job."

"Oh, I know he will. Have a good evening."

"And you."

The lady went on her way. Casey turned, looking at the thinning grey hair on the back of her head. Parts of her scalp were visible under the glaring lamp posts. Casey wondered what sound she'd make if she struck her with a rock, smashing it into her skull; she imagined the vivid blood seeping into the grey, and she smelled it, coppery and welcome.

6

NATALIE

When Scott and I met in university, we both wanted to be writers. His dream was to write historical novels and I was going to pen pulse-pounding thrillers. But then life happened, as it does: he graduated and went on to pursue his PGCE, and I took a job in an office, simply for the money, until the office job claimed more and more of my effort and attention. My writing aspirations began to fade, as aspirations often do: absent-mindedly, without any fanfare.

When I asked him if he thought a writing course would be a good idea, he said, "Nat, you know I'll always support you."

But that was a lie.

It was little things at first, the way he'd complain if I stayed up late to work on a story instead of coming to bed with him. "It's like I don't even have a wife." He'd hide my notebook, claiming he didn't know where it was, but I was careful to always leave it on my desk. Once, I arrived home to find him reading one my stories to his friend, Gary.

I didn't let them know I was there. Pressing myself against the wall, I listened as Scott made my words sound ridiculous. Or maybe they *were* ridiculous; it was an early draft. He spoke in a cutting, high-pitched way, mimicking me, and then both of them laughed like crazy.

"I'm telling you, mate," Scott said. "She spends hours on this crap."

Another woman might've marched in there and yelled at him for being so cruel. But my husband sometimes scared me. It was this look he got in his eyes, cruel, or hungry, like he wanted to hurt me but had so far held back the sadistic desire. I crept away, out the front door, walking to the end of the road before I let the tears come.

Perhaps he was right; perhaps I had no talent. But that didn't mean he had to mock me, to make me feel so worthless.

"Do you resent me for trying to be a writer?" I asked him once, when we were reading in bed.

He turned with that look I mentioned. Flinty eyes, a curling of his upper lip. "Seems like a strange question."

"Well... I'm asking."

"I don't resent you."

"But?"

"Who said there was a but?"

A tingle moved up my spine, an instinct. It was like I was waiting to be hit. Scott had never laid a hand on me. Our marriage was distant; emotionally speaking, he was never there, and when he did deign to share his feelings with me, he behaved as though he was doing me a favour. It was like I was somehow beneath him.

I summoned courage. This conversation needed to be had. "Sometimes I feel like you want me to fail because you've stopped trying. The writing course, Scott, it isn't..."

"What?" He leaned closer, laying his book in his lap. "Spit it out. Jesus."

"It's not a personal attack on you."

He laughed in that belittling way of his. I'd spotted it in the early days, but he'd had so many redeeming qualities. At least, he'd pretended to be loving and attentive and loyal. I was there when his dad died, and I saw how amazing he was with his mum, how affectionate and supportive.

But with the ring on my finger and the years passing, he was making less of an effort.

"I know it's not," he said after a pause. "What would you attack me with? Your little story? Give me a break."

I hated the sobbing that gripped me. It made me feel like a child. "I'm trying. That's more than I can say for you."

"Just leave me alone."

"Maybe I *will* leave you alone."

"A divorce? I'm praying for it. Put me out of my misery."

"You're a bitter failure," I snapped, leaping to my feet. I threw something. I wasn't sure what until it smashed against the wall, the hairdryer cracking, plastic shrapnel chipping away. "You wanted to be a historian. You failed. Then it was a writer. You failed. Every time you go for a promotion at work, they reject you. And you know why? Because they can tell how *evil* you are–"

"Shut the fuck up, bitch! Bitch!"

He raged from the room. I'd never seen him like this. I yelled and jumped out of his way when he almost barged into me. His footsteps pounded through the house, echoing through the walls, and headed down the hallway. Suddenly I knew where he was going.

I ran after him, reaching the door to my office just as he turned, my notebook in his hand.

"What are you doing?"

"Get out of my way." He strode right up to me, eyes blazing, crumpling the notebook in his trembling fist. "I mean it. Unless you want to share a bed with your bitch of a mum."

His words made me gasp. My mum had recently been in a car accident. She was going to be released the following day.

He pushed past me and went down the stairs. I chased him into the kitchen, as he went to the cooker and pressed down on the hob. The blue flame flickered to life. "Don't interfere," he said, when I raised my hand to stop him. But what was I going to do? "I mean it. I can't be fucked with this anymore. You prancing around the place, acting like you're better than me because you've done three weeks on a poxy writing course. It's pathetic."

The corner of the notebook made a crisping noise as it burned. Scott opened the back door and walked into the garden, the burning book the only point of light, the flames growing and shimmering in Scott's eyes, catching flashes of his smile; it peeled wider across his face, the more the book burned, and finally he let it drop onto the stones.

I think that was it, right then, the moment our marriage went from uncomfortable and unloving to outright vile. That was the moment I knew I was married to a monster.

7

SCOTT

Scott suppressed a yawn as the children filed out for lunchtime. It had taken several hours to clear up the mess Casey had made.

It was easier to break things than fix them, and really that was just perfect; like their marriage, it could be torn apart in one conversation and never pieced back together again. He'd spent the night thinking of his next move, deciding that visiting Natalie's parents was the best step he had available.

Her parents still lived in Natalie's childhood home. If the *hangman's tree* from her note referred to something in the local area, they'd know. Scott had googled it on his work computer, but he'd found nothing. If it was some local legend or anything like that, maybe there was no mention of it on the internet. He had to be sure.

The only problem was that meant seeing them for the first time since the funeral. It was no secret they blamed Scott for Natalie's death.

But Scott needed to solve the note. Perhaps the *we* in Natalie's final words would lead him to somebody who had answers; perhaps it was even Casey. She and Natalie's relationship could've gone far deeper than he knew. They could've been childhood friends. Whatever it was, he wasn't going to take this without a fight.

Big strong man, a voice whispered, mocking, fading. *Such a big tough guy, aren't you?*

The previous night, when Casey had finally returned home, she'd spent a long time walking around the house. Running her finger over every surface. Getting on her hands and knees to look under the sofa. Leaning close to the Aga as though hoping to find a remnant of sauce or a piece of glass from a shattered jar.

"Just about good enough," she'd declared, striding for the door. "You can have the sofa tonight."

Now, Scott dropped down behind his desk, burying his face in his hands. He heard Lauren approach slowly. Scott had expected things to be awkward after Casey sent her the dick pic, but Lauren had been professional, focusing on the kids.

"Are you all right?" she asked.

He looked up. She was a few years younger than him, in her mid-twenties, with a bob of blonde hair. She always dressed smartly, in pleated trousers and a buttoned-up shirt. She had a hipster look about her. "I meant what I said about the you-know-what. So I hope it isn't that."

"It's..." He waited as she sat. He couldn't tell her, could he? They had only ever discussed school matters. "I'm seeing Natalie's parents later. It's the first time since her funeral."

"Why?"

"Why am I seeing them or why is it the first time?"

She shrugged. "Both."

From beyond the classroom, sounds of lunchtime reached them: yelling and music played from phones and one of his colleagues calling for somebody to slow down.

"I'm seeing them because... well, it's the right thing to do."

That wasn't entirely a lie; it was the right thing to do for his investigation. *Investigation.* It was a joke. "And the reason it's been so long is they're horrible. I know that's a terrible thing to say about your dead wife's parents, but... At Natalie's funeral, her mother refused to speak. She said it was all well and good attending, but she wouldn't grace a suicide with loving words."

That was Theresa, and she didn't even know the full truth.

Scott picked up his stress ball, gave it a good squeeze. "Can you believe that? That's how she phrased it."

"That's messed up. Are you sure it's not anything else? I don't mean to pry."

For a second, Scott thought about telling her. At least then she'd understand why he had massive bags under his eyes. And why he'd found it even more difficult today to put up with Beth Vaughn's crap. She was one of his year eleven students and by far the most disruptive. Scott sensed she didn't have the best home life. Like a lot of troubled kids, Beth hid behind a shield of sarcasm and cruelty to deal with it.

But he didn't know Lauren. They weren't friends.

"That's it," he said. "Trust me. That's bad enough."

"You can speak to me. If you need to."

"Can I? Why?" His tone was too snappy. He couldn't help it. "My personal problems aren't your concern."

"Maybe I could help."

"With Natalie's parents? I highly doubt that."

Lauren fiddled with her bracelet. "You seem a little distracted today. That's all. As long as it isn't about the you-know-what."

Scott looked around the room, laughing darkly when he saw they were alone and the hallway was empty; in a busy school, it was always wise to check. "Dick pic, Lauren. You can say it. I sent you a photo of my dick by accident because I'm an idiot who should've thought about what he was doing before he did it."

He'd fallen for Casey so easily. The first night had been like a scene from a porn film, Casey taking the lead as she did everything a man could wish for, as she asked for nothing in return. Grinning like a man who'd recently hit his head – who didn't understand there was a bleed on his brain – he'd taken everything she offered.

His fist was tight around the stress ball. Lauren was talking. He focused past the haze. "Sorry?"

"I said you shouldn't be so hard on yourself. You made a mistake."

"Yeah."

"I already told you, it's fine."

"Thank you," he said. "I mean that."

But it wouldn't be fine until Casey backed off. Nothing would.

8

SCOTT

"Thanks for asking for my permission, honey," Casey said down the phone. Scott was squeezing it hard, pressing it forcefully against his ear. "It's honestly so thoughtful. And yes, of course you can go and see Natalie's parents. I'd never stand in the way of that. I just hope you remember what we talked about."

Did she think he was recording this conversation? He hadn't thought of that, though he saw it would be a good idea. Get her to reveal the monster behind the mask.

"I won't forget. Don't worry."

"Okay, great. I love you."

"I love you too," he said, forcing the words out.

"I love you *more*."

Were they really doing this?

It turned out they were. For at least a minute, they went through the routine, talking like they were teenage lovers. In the end, Casey magnanimously admitted Scott loved her more.

Once she'd hung up, he took a moment, breathing slowly. She knew she had all the power; she knew she could tell him to come home right now and he would. She must've guessed his planned visit had something to do with her blackmail. The timing was too coincidental. So why was she letting him go?

Maybe she was that confident in her control. Maybe she didn't care. Maybe she thought he was going to fail, no matter what his plan was.

Scott ignored the little voice telling him she was right. He often wondered if he thought he deserved this, or something like it, deep down. As if he'd earned payback for a wrong he didn't even know he'd committed. Like he was guilty.

Stuffing his emotions away – he was good at that – he drove out of Bristol, taking the motorway to Weston-super-Mare. He tried to listen to the audiobook he'd started the previous week, but the words kept jumbling in his mind. The narrator's voice became Casey's syrupy confidence, mocking him, humiliating him, until he had to switch it off.

He focused on the road, not letting himself think about how futile this was. There was no indication that Natalie's suicide note had anything to do with Casey. But he had to try.

He hadn't rung ahead, not wanting to risk Natalie's parents hanging up on him. He doubted they wanted to see him. They'd hardly looked at him at the funeral, as though blaming him for the way Natalie had died: blaming him for their daughter becoming a sinner.

Walking up their neat front garden, he paused at the front door. He raised his hand. Lowered it. Raised it again. He thought of their faces, the resentment in their eyes. He couldn't do this; he had to go.

The door swung open.

"What are you doing here?" Harvey glared, his hand on the door frame, a man as neat as his garden with a meticulous comb-over and a smart sweatshirt.

"I... I need to talk about Natalie."

"Why?"

"She left a note, Harvey. I'm sorry. I should've told you."

Harvey took a step forward. Scott flinched away, certain for a mad second the man was going to punch him.

But he was doing a witness check. Scott had heard the phrase in a documentary he and Casey had watched. *Snuggled up on the sofa, so in love it hurt.*

A witness check was when criminals looked around to make sure nobody was watching. Harvey didn't want anybody overhearing anything about his daughter. He didn't want anybody seeing Scott. It was a crime, Scott being here.

"Come in," Harvey snapped, "before Theresa gets home."

Scott had teased Natalie about her mother's name. Whenever she did something to upset Natalie, Scott would say, "Hey, don't talk about Mother Theresa like that." It was one of their old jokes, repeated many times over the years, and it always made her smile. *Well, not always.*

He followed Harvey; there were no photos of Natalie hanging from the walls in the hallway, or on the display cabinet in the living room. There was no sign of her at all.

Harvey didn't offer to make Scott a cup of tea. He sat and gestured for Scott to take the opposite chair. "What did the note say?"

"I've got to say, Harvey, I thought you'd be more surprised."

"I must apologise, profusely, for not living up to your expectations. In this note, did she apologise?"

"To who?"

Harvey looked at him with dead seriousness. There was no irony in his expression at all. "To God."

Scott envied and hated him. To have such conviction. "No, she didn't. And she didn't need to. She could've said sorry to me. To you. To Theresa. To her friends. She doesn't owe God anything."

"That's blasphemy."

Scott shrugged. "I guess it is."

"You've been in my home a minute, if that."

"So?"

"You're already wearing my patience thin. It's been terribly difficult for me and my wife to move on. But, with a lot of prayer and patience, we're slowly getting there. We could do without your disrespect."

Harvey's voice shook towards the end, his cheeks colouring red. Suddenly Scott saw him for what he was. A grieving father, a man who was dealing with his loss in the only way he knew how.

"I'm sorry," Scott said. "I didn't mean to disrespect you. I could've done this over the phone–"

"I can assure you, we would have preferred that. Theresa is due home in fifteen minutes. Please hurry up."

"All right then." Scott recited the note from memory. "The hangman's broken tree. Does that ring any bells?"

"Isn't the note addressed to you?"

"It wasn't addressed to anybody."

"But isn't it *for* you? Surely you should know what she's talking about."

Scott shook his head. "I–"

"Because the thing is, Scott, and I'm sorry if I seem a little abrasive. But the thing is... you *should* know. Natalie was your wife. One flesh, young man, one flesh. It sounds like you're telling me there was somebody else in Natalie's life, somebody you didn't know about."

"That's what I'm trying to–"

"Which would make *you* partly to blame. At least." Harvey aimed his finger as though he thought Scott would catch on fire and he liked the idea. "Your wife–"

"What about your bloody daughter?" Scott cut in. "I can't

see a single photo of her. It's like you've wiped her out of fucking existence."

Harvey threw his hands up. "What a civilised man you are, swearing at your father-in-law."

"You're not my father-in-law."

"That's right. Because you moved on before your wife was even cold."

"She's never going to be cold though, is she? According to you, she's burning for all eternity."

"You're a theologian now as well as a wife killer, is that it?"

Scott leapt to his feet, raised his fist, looming over the old man. Harvey's mouth dropped open as he stared up. Scott paused when he realised what he was doing; he never normally allowed his temper to flare like that. *Big tough man, Scott.*

He took a step back, shaking his head. "Please, just tell me if you know what she's talking about. Was there a place she used to go to as a kid? Maybe she'd meet her friends there?"

"I don't see why I should tell you anything after the way you've behaved."

"I'm sorry. All right? I'm sorry she's dead and I'm sorry I didn't know she was going to do it. I'm sorry I didn't see the signs and I know it's my fault. I should've known something was wrong. But I didn't. I failed her."

"You're right. You did."

Harvey's hand went to his chest, presumably to where his cross lay beneath the fabric of his jumper. He looked almost serene for a moment.

"There's a tree in Hope Grounds, in the top corner. It's grown crooked in the wind. It leans against the railing. You can't miss it. The children would joke that it used to be a hangman's tree and it broke when a particularly heavy victim was killed there. A rather nasty joke, in my view. Is there anything else?"

"No. Thank you." Scott walked over to the door, paused. "I loved her, you know. I still love her."

It was the truth, no matter what had happened. Despite all the... the *shit*. Scott had always loved Natalie.

"I'm sure you believe that," Harvey said. "But if you did, she wouldn't be dead. You would've spotted the signs. You would've made sure she got help. And now she's doomed, like you said. You can mock me all you want. It's the truth. She's doomed, and it's all your fault."

Scott ducked his head and strode down the hallway. Harvey was blaming a husband for his wife's death – a death that had almost ruined Scott – when *he* was the one at fault.

And yet that wasn't true. Scott could've helped her, been better in certain ways. But it was ridiculous, the way Harvey and Theresa behaved. Disowning their own daughter, destroying any trace of her in their homes. No photos. No concern. Just forget her; put her in the ground and leave her there to rot. And they only knew her as the daughter, an angel. How could they ever reject that, *her*?

Scott stopped when he saw the vigil. From a side room off the hallway – it had been Harvey's small office the last time Scott was here – dozens of photos were displayed in gold and silver frames, unlit candles sitting beneath them.

Natalie was smiling as a little girl and waving as a teenager and caught mid-laugh as a young woman. She was beaming on their wedding day and grinning as she held onto her mother's hand on the beach. Scott walked into the room.

She was beautiful; her smile brought to mind dozens of memories, all of them clashing, their first kiss and her low voice whispering in his ear. *I think I love you.* He'd laughed and pulled her closer, both of them drunk, both of them not caring, knowing they could do anything.

Scott was bloody crying again.

Behind him, Harvey's footsteps. Scott turned, expecting anger, but Harvey only frowned softly. "I suppose both of us could've handled that better."

Scott snorted back an ugly-sounding sob. "Yeah, I'd say so."

Harvey sighed. "We'll never stop loving her. Even if we disagree with what she did."

Harvey visibly hesitated for a moment, but then he pulled Scott into a hug. Scott wrapped his arms around the older man and embraced him gratefully. They stayed like that for a time, then Harvey took a step back. "Please, before Theresa..."

"I understand. Do you want to know if I find anything?"

Harvey looked at the vigil. "No, we've got everything we need. Don't visit unannounced again."

Scott left the house and walked across the street.

9

NATALIE

I knew Scott had a temper right from the beginning. When we first met in university, he'd get sulky if things didn't go his way. Sometimes – especially if he'd been drinking – this sulkiness would become something else. He'd rant about the tiniest thing, like a drink being late, or his food order being wrong. Once a man hit on me in a club and Scott left, sending me a text from outside.

I can't believe you'd do this to me.

I rang him and he told me he was waiting around the corner. I found him leaning against a wall in a nearby alleyway, his knuckles covered in blood. The wheelie bin was smeared in crimson, looking black and sticky.

I was an idiot; I took this display to mean he truly cared about me, to mean he was passionate and wanted me all to himself. In a sick way, I sort of liked it. It was evidence of how devoted he was, how deep his feelings ran.

A smarter person – or a person less in love – would've taken that as a warning. She would've backed off, or at the very least told him that kind of behaviour was unacceptable. But I didn't.

I held him, whispering it was okay. I wasn't interested in anybody except him.

"You'll never cheat on me, will you?" He held me so tight. It was still affection, I told myself. Even if he was squeezing just a little too hard. He wasn't threatening me. "I couldn't handle that, Nat. I'd go insane."

"Never. I swear."

He felt freer to express his anger after we were married. We had a chore list which we'd agreed upon, splitting the tasks evenly throughout the week. If Scott missed one of his chores, it was acceptable; work was stressful and he couldn't summon the motivation to hoover the living room. But if *I* missed one, he'd look around the flat, sneering, as though any messiness was a personal affront.

"Do you want us to live in a shithole?" he roared one time.

Spinning, he smashed his fist into the wall, caving it in. He tore off the canvas painting and tried to snap it over his knee, failed, then threw it at the wall instead. He strode over to me, his chest heaving, his eyes alight just like they'd been when he burned my notebook.

I cringed away, hating the sound of my voice: small, weak. Not at all like I'd sounded before we got married. "I'm sorry. I forgot. I'll sort it."

"You better."

I didn't ask him what would happen if I didn't.

Sometimes, he'd get this look in his eyes after throwing one of his tantrums. As he stared at me, it was like I could hear the flow of his thoughts. *Hit her hit her hit her.* His fists trembling, a strange twist to his lips – something between a smile and a grimace, as though he was getting excited but wasn't confident enough yet – he'd walk right up to me. He'd stop. He'd catch himself.

Rage would turn to love, and he'd start crying, holding me and telling me he was sorry.

10

SCOTT

Scott walked across the park.

It was built with one side facing a residential housing estate, the back gardens separated by a stone wall. Scott didn't envy the people who lived in those houses, where anybody could scale the wall and get access to their property.

One of the things he loved about his house was the privacy, with its tall hedges, detached so no nosy neighbours could get involved in his business.

The hangman's broken tree was easy to find, right where Harvey had said it would be. A giant with its lower branches twisting through the railing, it looked like a drunken man who'd taken a stumble. Scott waved at a dogwalker as he approached it, trying his best to smile.

He walked around the tree, inspecting the trunk, looking for any signs of a carving.

A few passers-by gave him odd looks. Scott ignored them and walked around the tree several times. He couldn't see anything. He ran his hands over the bark, thinking maybe he could feel some faint indentations.

He wasn't sure he wanted to find anything.

There was a fact he'd been ignoring ever since he found the note: if Natalie had addressed a note to somebody else, she may have been having an affair.

Scott couldn't imagine that.

Can't you? Fucking idiot?

Natalie had been happy with their life. She had a well-paying job as a manager at a car insurance company. She was following her passion for writing on the side, attending classes, writing short stories and working on longer pieces. They had as much romance in their relationship as any other couple, Scott thought; they did their best.

Her suicide had hit him violently, suddenly, without warning.

As he circled the tree another time, he thought about Natalie coming here with her lover. It must've been so exciting for them, rushing through the park, their hands all over each other. Maybe they'd even had sex up against this tree. Maybe Scott was standing on the very spot his wife had betrayed him.

It was no use. There was nothing.

He leaned against the tree, hands in his pockets, muttering the note's words. "Down by the hangman's broken tree..."

By the tree. She hadn't said she'd carved it *on* the tree.

He studied the nearby trees, the railing, and finally came to the stone wall that separated the park from the houses. It was just about tall enough so he couldn't see into their gardens, but not by much.

He walked up and down the wall.

And there it was.

"Jesus."

He ran his thumb over his wife's name.

Natalie and–

Somebody had destroyed the other name, scratching at the stone until it was a mess, the word lost beneath it: rubbing with

47

such force that the name was more than obliterated, a large chunk taken out of the flimsy brickwork. Perhaps it was Natalie's lover, and they'd had a fight before Natalie's death.

Scott warned himself to slow down; he didn't know anything yet.

But it wasn't looking good.

Natalie and *who*?

Scott realised a truth. He'd known it for a long time. Tucked away. Roared out of existence. Where it could be easily ignored.

His first wife was as much of a stranger as his second.

11

SCOTT

He knew this was probably going to lead nowhere. But he didn't want to return to Bristol without learning something concrete. He walked up the pathway; this garden was far less neat than Harvey's, with two children's bikes lying on the grass, a football net that had come loose from the frame, tangled up in the corner. The grass was overgrown and there was a drawing in the window, a smiling rainbow.

It was the house which overlooked the hangman's broken tree: which overlooked the place Natalie might have met her lover. If it was a lover. Perhaps it had been a friend. Or was that wishful thinking? He needed to find out.

He honestly did feel stupid though, both for not following this up sooner and for how strange this would seem to whoever answered this door. *Pretend you're in a play.* His mum had used to say that to him, as a kid, when his dad was on one of his furies: rampaging, angry about work, breaking things and raging chaotically around the house.

He knocked on the door. Immediately a dog started to yap, low and protective. "Bailey!" a woman yelled. "Bailey! Enough!"

The door opened and a woman stepped forward. She was holding a tea towel in one hand and her other was spattered in soap. "I asked you to ring me when you were here." When Scott didn't answer, she said, "Aren't you the delivery driver?"

"No, I'm sorry."

"Then what..."

This was so stupid. He didn't know how to start. "I noticed your house overlooks the park."

"Right."

"I needed to speak to you about something."

He sounded like a weirdo perv.

She wiped her hand on the tea towel and then folded her arms. "Right."

"Well, I think my wife might've scrawled her name on the wall." Jesus *Christ*; when he heard himself say it, he wanted to run away. "I was wondering if you'd ever seen her here before, possibly with another person?"

"I don't understand."

"My wife–"

"I don't spend all day looking out my window. Two kids, a dog who drives me up the wall. Are you bloody serious?"

Scott swallowed. "I think my wife was having an affair. Her name is carved into the wall directly behind your house. There's another name too, but somebody scratched it away. I was wondering if you'd ever seen her."

A look passed across the woman's face; she was thinking of something. It was curiosity and then eyes widening as something hit her, then a smile like she'd just won one hundred pounds on a lottery ticket, then her expression hardened. She wanted nothing to do with it. But there was something.

"What is it?" Scott asked, thinking maybe Harvey was right after all; he wished he had a cross to touch, for an odd second, when he'd never wanted that before. Not even with Natalie.

"I'm not in the habit of helping blokes spy on their wives," the woman said after a long pause.

Scott took a step forward when she made to shut the door. "But you know something."

"Are you going to be a problem?" She gestured down the hallway – past dozens of children's and dog's toys – to a big bulldog, presumably Bailey. Bailey was sitting a few feet away, teeth bared, barking replaced with a low rumbling growl.

"No." Scott moved away. "I swear. It's not like that."

"No, then what's it like?"

"She killed herself. My wife. She mentioned the hangman's tree in her note. I think whoever she was here with, they might know something..."

The woman sighed, glancing into her house, looking at Scott again. "Do you have any idea how weird this is?"

"I know."

"Listen, all right... I do know something. But I don't want you coming back here. You can't go around knocking on people's doors at all times of the day just because you feel like it."

Scott suddenly wanted to apologise to Mikey Hutton, who he'd scolded last week in almost this exact same manner. She had it right down to the subtle disgust, just enough to make him feel like a total arse. "Yeah, I get that."

She shook her head, looking down at the tea towel in her hand. *Big man Scott gets what he wants when he wants.*

"When we first moved in," the lady said, "the estate agent explained about the park. She said it was quiet most of the time. *That* was a lie, let me tell you. But anyway... she mentioned the names. She said she could arrange to have them removed, since it's technically on our wall. It don't bother me. It's on the other side. But I guess some people complained before, when she was showing them the house and the park and that. Mental. I don't understand it. But she said it, and then, guess what..."

Scott waited.

"She tried to *charge* me. Can you believe that? If I wanted it removed!"

The lady laughed. Scott laughed with her, glad the big dog had stopped growling.

"I never saw her. Your wife, I mean. We only moved in a year ago. But the estate agent did. She made a joke about it."

"What joke?"

"Listen, I don't want anything to do with it. It's none of my business. I need to get on with dinner."

"Please just give me something. Please."

"I don't–"

"I found her. I found Natalie. That was my wife's name." *Big man Scott going to cry.* "I was the one who found her in the garage. And it'll never leave me. I'll never forget it."

"Why not just leave it alone?" the woman said; there was something sad, and a little hateful in her eyes.

"Because you obviously have something to say."

"I know what the estate agent said. This is none of my business."

"Can you at least give me the name of the estate agent? Please?"

The woman stared at him for a long time. Bailey started grumbling again. Beyond the dog, a TV was playing, a newscaster explaining something about the economy. It seemed so normal, messy, full of life.

"It's Royal Lettings, in town. The lady's name was Rachel. I remember because we used to call her Rachel Roy*al*. Like a Roy*ale* with cheese. You seen that one?"

"Uh, I think so."

She shut the door and Scott walked back down the path, the woman's words ricocheting around his mind. Whatever the estate agent had said, it had clearly been something about his wife. Sitting in his car, he thought about God, thought about the love he'd felt in his early years, with Dad, Mum and him in church, the atmosphere of it, the optimism, like he was being filled with light.

University – and reason – had bred religion out of him. Plus he'd seen its weakness in his dad, doing nothing to stop against the drink, and all the clichéd crap it brought. His father's job had been his life, and any failure in that meant his life was over. That was how he'd felt. And he'd never hit Scott, nor his mother. But Scott had always felt as if he was waiting.

Maybe he'd been waiting for this. To be put in his place.

No. That couldn't be right.

Be right, as if there was a plan, and yet he couldn't deny the allure right now. All his sensibilities were for the physical, the tactile world and inferences made on evidence; he sometimes wished he'd become a professor, or perhaps studied archaeology, but he truly enjoyed teaching secondary school. That was why he'd resisted taking on head-of-year positions; he relished focusing on his class.

You're a bitter failure. They can tell how evil you are–

His phone rang.

Casey.

Maybe he wouldn't answer. But what if that spurred her to send another photo?

"Hello."

"Hey, sweetie. Are you going to be much longer?"

"I'm on my way home."

"Excellent! I thought you might like to make dinner tonight. I've already bought all the ingredients. But you don't have to."

As if he was going to believe that. "I'd love to."

"I *knew* you would. Just don't be longer than an hour, okay? I might get bored and start looking for things to do."

Scott picked up his pace; he hadn't missed the warning.

12

CASEY

Casey knew Scott had been up to something. Maybe he was thinking of a way to fight back.

Fight back like teddies an army with swords in their hands and Goliath is looming his shadow and his voice is booming and—

Casey took a moment to compose herself as Scott walked through the kitchen door.

Her focus was sharp, like a lance, but her horse was unsteady; she thought that made sense. She almost laughed. She'd rolled Gorilla Glue and then two sativa-dominant strains, Lemon Haze and Stardawg into a big chunky joint, with just enough tobacco to make it burn nicely. She'd achieved exactly the effect she wanted.

She was always in control. Had been ever since the iron. *A snake goes hiss, now give me a kiss.* She paced over to Scott; her mind annoyed her sometimes.

As she patted him down head to toe – she wouldn't let him record her; she hated being filmed – she wondered what pathetic plan he'd concocted. Whatever it was, it would fail.

She had the kill switch. She could erase his entire life with the push of a button. She had the nuclear motherfucking codes.

So let him try. See if it worked. It would only make it more fun; that was the point, the only truly honest thing in this world.

The pursuit of something other than... than the emptiness, the death in the puddle which stares at a person as they are standing still, leaking memories which were never formed, experiences never lived. Casey was not like other people.

And if things went too far, she could easily rein him in.

Taking his phone, she checked it wasn't recording and then placed it on the table. "Great. Now you can get dinner started."

He raised his eyebrow as he moved from the dining area to the kitchen. It was an open-plan space, but not small like the flat Casey had lived in before snagging Scott. It had a tall ceiling and a giant table and a big Aga oven. It was the sort of place a man could afford when he had his daddy's inheritance to spunk away; if Casey had only wanted money from this wretch, she would've gutted the little prick the day he said *I do*.

"What am I making?" he asked.

"Turkish lamb dumplings. Do you remember the last time you made them?"

He winced. Good memories probably hurt him. They meant nothing to Casey. They'd never been good or bad. They'd all been a part of her plan, her one-year magnificent genius scheme. She was feeling *good*. A gorilla was gluing her bones together, easing any pain, there was a lemony taste to her thoughts, and a dog made of stars barked annoyingly in her mind, begging to have the constellations in its throat cut.

Scott was taking a very long time to respond. Or maybe it was the funny and interesting things happening to time. "I remember."

"You were so excited to make it, like a little kid on Christmas Day. Then you ruined it and we had to order pizza. That was a wonderful night, wasn't it?"

He did his annoying teeth-grinding thing. "Yeah, it was."

"Well then." She clapped her hands. "Better get started. I'll be in the living room."

She dropped onto the sofa and clicked play on her phone, the music filtering through the Bluetooth speakers. It was a pop mix, songs from when she was a teenager.

She'd run around her bedroom with a hairbrush in her hand, wondering if *he* would leave her alone today; she'd disappear into fantasies of being a pop star, crowds screaming her name. Every few minutes, she'd check the front window for her dad's car, just in case. It would be time to turn the music down then.

As she listened, she looked over her adoring fans, all of them yelling, reaching out for her, desperate for a piece of her. She bobbed her head and opened her mouth, singing softly.

And then she thought about Scott, the *real* Scott. The phrase made her so tingly.

Real Scott.

There was a fake version of him, the one he pretended to be at school and with his friends and everybody else. Then there was the genuine version, the beast he hid from the rest of the world.

The *issues*. There were no issues. She was in the right. This was her prize. She'd worked for this.

Her thoughts were doing something annoying. They were fracturing, little vines pulling memories up from places best left forgotten. There was a long white sock with a bloody tooth sticking to the end of it, and a mug with a faded love heart on it, a crack down the middle, and somebody was yelling but their voice was a kiss and a tingle cut down her back and split her spine in two.

She opened her eyes and sat up. This wasn't helping anybody or anything.

It was time for distraction.

She returned to the kitchen to find Scott staring down at a

tray of burnt goo. He looked like he was going to cry again. It hardly looked real, the way his eyes got all glassy so fast, like he was a toy with a string hanging from his back.

Casey giggled. "Have you ruined dinner, darling?"

"I..."

"Ruined dinner?"

"I ruined dinner." He raised his hands, as though he thought she was going to attack him. "But I can fix it."

She gestured to the tray. "With everything on the line, you couldn't even cook a simple meal."

"It's hardly a simple meal, is it?"

"What a tone to take with your wife." She walked around the kitchen divider, swished her hips as she got closer. She was wearing her dressing gown and her body tingled when she saw how difficult he found it to resist her, even now, the sick bastard. "But you've always had women to cook for you, haven't you? First your mummy and then Natalie at university and then me."

"I can cook," he said. "Just not complicated stuff."

"What *are* we going to do about this?"

He wanted so badly to be a tough guy. He was looking at her like he might start swinging. She wouldn't have cared if he did. She'd left her phone in the living room. That was a problem, considering what she'd done the previous night; all part of the fun though, plus she could always change it back.

Passcode. And a tingle strummed in her, the string of an instrument. She was finally part of the drama somebody of her unique intellect deserved. She was filling it, stuffing it all in, right in the nothing; there was sensation, where before there had been only the absence of light.

"I know!" Casey turned to the Aga and switched on the boiler plate. "Be a dear and pop your hand down there. Don't take it away until I tell you to."

Casey was so fucking doing this.

"You've got to be joking," Scott said.

Casey sighed dramatically, making it last a long time, properly huffing and puffing. "You're boring me. You know how this ends. Don't make me say it."

"But–"

"*Fine*. Put your fucking hand on the fucking boiling plate before I release every fucking video I fucking have. Clear enough?"

"Casey, please."

"Casey, please," she imitated, whiny and annoying. Laughing, she gestured at the Aga. "Tick-tock."

"I can't."

"You can. You will."

She stared at him, and she knew he wasn't the sort of man who could stand up to her. There was something so pathetically willing in his little doll's eyes, the fake-looking fuck, staring at her as though she owed him something. After all the times she'd choked on this man's dick, all the times he'd stuck it in her ass, then grinned at her like a complete moron. *Oh my God, Casey, that was so crazy.*

Little naïve pathetic loser.

"Are you going to make me tell you again?" she snapped.

And then – *hiss*, it was going to *hiss* – he really did it. He pressed his hand down and started whining. Casey was sure she could smell flesh cooking, could hear the *hiss* of iron–

Of his flesh, and she found herself wanting him, for the first time since their marriage. Not the other Casey, but the real her; she stared at how utterly beautiful he looked as the *hiss* serenaded her.

Her body sparkled and she knew she'd touch herself later.

He snatched his hand away. "Jesus Christ."

"Tut-tut. I didn't ask you to stop."

"Please."

"Scottie, darling..."

"Can I use my other hand, at least?"

"No, you can't. Now do what you're told."

When he hesitated, Casey darted her hand out and curled it around his wrist. He didn't fight her; he let her guide him, pushing his palm down on the plate.

She was in charge and nobody could tell her otherwise. Scott deserved this and nobody could ever argue with that. They were facts as true as the sun rising, as the colour of grass, the depth of the ocean.

When his moaning started to ruin it – he'd need a gag if he wanted to whine that loudly – she let his wrist go.

"Shall we order pizza?" she said.

Scott took a step back and opened his mouth. He was about to shout at her.

She gave him a look; she wasn't going to let him disrespect her.

"Sure." He stared down at his burnt hand. "Pizza sounds good."

His tone was so goddamn annoying, threatening to ruin her high. It was the weakness of it; that was the worst part. He wanted the wife who did what he wanted all the time, but he was too scared to fight for it. He was truly, unquestionably, without a single doubt – and obvious to anybody who'd spent even thirty seconds with him – a pussy.

Casey remembered once in school, screaming that at the so-called bully as she held a bunch of her ugly bleached hair in her hand, staring down at her. *What are you going to do now, pussy?* And the same word, in another place, but it was power; this was power.

She had the blood of a lion and the scars of a warrior.

"Go on then," she said, as she strode into the hallway.

"Don't get the order wrong. You should know what I like by now."

"So that part was real, was it? That's our whole marriage? Ham and pineapple pizza?"

He said it to himself, but he was speaking loudly, a passive-aggressive way to make her hear it but so he could still deny it later.

And maybe *later* she'd find something else then, if the selfish dick wanted to play that game.

For now, she went into the living room and sat down, turned up the music, and graced the crowd with her voice.

13

SCOTT

"What happened to your hand, Scott?"

He looked up at Lauren. She was standing over his desk, her arms folded, staring like an accuser. Maybe Lauren was secretly working with Casey. Maybe she was about to pull out a hammer and take it to his goddamn head. His hand was hot fire; he'd bought some salve on the way to school, wrapped it in a bandage, but that was it. He might need to go to hospital.

But would Casey let him?

Let him. He wanted to flip the bloody desk.

"Scott?"

"I burned it by mistake."

He wondered, in a distant sort of way, if he qualified as a beaten husband now. The thought almost made him laugh.

Lauren unfolded her arms as she sat. Beyond them it was the school sounds, each one more annoying than usual. The wailing and the shouting and the music and the sense of being young and hopeful. But they'd see. All their dreams would turn to shit.

"I want to say something, but I don't want to offend you."

"Go ahead."

"You're acting weird. You have been all day. You're not paying attention. It's like you're somewhere else."

He was. He was in the kitchen, his hand pushed against the boiling plate, the agony, the sheer terrifying violence of it. He was watching Casey, as her smile spread wider.

"I'm fine."

"If something's wrong, we can talk about it."

"Why do you care?"

"Your job affects mine," she said. "The school's budget is rubbish as it is. You know that. If you go, I doubt they'll keep me around for the sake of it."

"If I go? As in, get fired? That seems a tad dramatic."

"You're not your usual self. First the picture. Now this. You've been staring at your hand half the day."

He couldn't deny that. He'd found himself gazing at the bandage far too often, remembering the glint in Casey's eyes. Pleasure like he'd never seen, nothing like the way she looked at him during sex.

There was a vicious creature locked inside his wife's body, and it only fed on pain. It wasn't like him and Natalie, the good mixed in with the bad; this was a knife produced from a bouquet of flowers and driven deep into his guts where all his ignored goddamn feelings were buried. *Fuck.*

He stared at his hand, warning himself to calm down. "Yeah, well."

"Yeah, well... what?"

He sighed. "You're coming on pretty strong."

She adjusted her bracelet. It was a stylish piece, with a studded silver tree on it. "Says the man who sent me a photo of his dick."

Scott laughed. It came from nowhere, and it felt good, a valve releasing pressure. "Fair enough."

They paused, Lauren sitting back, letting her hands drop.

Scott studied her, looking at her as the person instead of the teaching assistant. She'd always kept things professional. But she seemed genuinely shaken by his sudden change in mood.

"I can tell you what's going on," he said, "but you have to promise to never, ever tell anybody else."

Nothing to ruin that won't ruin you. There was never an us.

"I don't—"

"You have to promise. To swear. I love this job too much." He looked around the classroom, at the posters, a memory attached to them all. One timeline belonged to a student who was in university now, studying history, who'd even returned a few times to help out with after-school activities whenever he was back in Bristol. That meant something more than money.

"Okay, fine. I promise I won't tell anybody."

Scott told her everything – about him and Casey, not *everything* – starting at the beginning, on their anniversary night. He made sure to stress Casey had been the one to send the photo of his dick; that alone was enough of a reason to tell Lauren, so she knew with certainty he wasn't a creep. He finished with the boiler plate.

Lauren sat back, her hands on her knees.

"Aren't you going to ask me if it's a joke?"

"It does sound far-fetched."

Scott nodded. "No arguments there. I feel like I've walked into *Dr Jekyll and Mr Hyde*. It's like she's flipped a switch."

She frowned. "I've heard of this sort of situation before, but never like this, never just..."

"Just there," Scott said bitterly. "One day, when I got home. A new woman sitting in her place. I swear, I thought maybe it was Casey's twin. Part of me still thinks that."

"We're really living in a simulation if that's true."

Scott laughed gruffly, not even a laugh, just pushing air out. "Yeah."

"So what's your plan?"

"Aren't you going to tell me to go to the police?"

"No. The second she hears sirens, she's sending those photos."

"Yep."

Lauren sat forwards. "So?"

"I'm looking into Natalie's suicide note, which I should've done a long time ago. And I need to start looking into Casey too. But the thing is, if she hears about me snooping around, there's nothing stopping her from releasing the videos."

"Maybe it wouldn't be that bad," Lauren said. "This isn't the fifties or whatever. People are more accepting these days."

"Yeah, sure. But nobody wants their kids around somebody they've seen naked. That's just a basic fact. Even if they know I didn't do anything wrong – even if they know this was done *to* me – they wouldn't care."

Lauren nodded. "Let me help then. Casey doesn't know me. I'm sure there's something I can do."

Scott looked at her closely, to see if she was serious. She was a young woman with a life of her own, presumably with friends and family and hobbies. A partner, a pet cat if he remembered correctly. It struck Scott how little he knew about this person. Perhaps he was rude; perhaps he was too used to being trapped inside his own head.

"Why, Lauren?"

"What sort of person would I be if I didn't help?"

"A normal one. Most people wouldn't want anything to do with this."

"Maybe I'm not most people."

Scott thought for a moment. There might be something she could do to help. He wasn't in a position where he could turn it down.

"Casey quit the book club soon after we got together. It was awkward, for obvious reasons."

Lauren nodded; she didn't need him to tell her Casey and Natalie had attended the same book club. The school grapevine had taken care of that.

"The ladies there would recognise me. They'd get suspicious if I started asking questions about Casey."

"But they don't know me," Lauren said. "Okay. Let's do it."

Scott almost asked her why again, but he decided against it. She was offering to help. That was enough. Dimly, he thought of Harvey and his cross, and he wished he'd asked him to light the vigil. He thought – and he'd never share this with anyone – that perhaps, if he'd grown into a different man, he might see Lauren's willingness as a sign. An angel, driven by providence.

Opening and closing his hand, the bandage rubbed against the broken skin of his palm.

He was such an idiot.

14

SCOTT

After work, Scott sat in his car, his phone ringing through the loudspeaker system. The kids filed out in groups, a couple of the older ones casually lighting up cigarettes the second they were beyond the gates, even more sucking on colourful vape pens. Scott recognised Beth Vaughn, with her bleached blonde hair and one of the boy's arms wrapped around her; it had been a different boy the previous week.

As Scott watched, both of them sparked up, smoking as one of their friends pulled a wheely on his bike next to them. Scott wasn't judging Beth. As far as he was concerned, women could have as many partners as they wanted. He didn't care. But Beth wasn't a woman; she was a child. And he knew what she was doing. Seeking approval in the worst places, going down the wrong path.

It had happened with a couple of his previous students. That was the thing with being a teacher. Scott saw the cycles. One girl, exactly like Beth, now had two children with two different fathers, both absent. Scott had seen her around, heard her story from another teacher. She never looked happy. She seemed to hate her children. Scott felt sorry for all three of them.

If anything, it was the boys that made Scott the angriest. Teenagers could be grim when it came to the opposite sex. He'd overheard some nasty stuff. Once he'd suspended a student for roughly yanking on a girl's bra strap.

The phone stopped ringing. "Good afternoon, Royal Lettings, Ellie speaking, how can I help?"

"Yes, hello. I was wondering if Rachel's working today."

"Can I ask what this is in regard to?"

"Uh, one of her houses."

"Is it a maintenance issue? We've recently moved our services onto an online portal—"

"It's not. Please, I need to speak with her."

Ellie paused. Scott imagined her making a face at one of her colleagues. "Sure, I'll connect you."

"Thank you."

A moment later, Rachel came through. "Hello, how can I help?"

"Hi, Rachel. My name is Scott." He wasn't sure how to start. "I need to talk to you about twenty-seven Park Avenue."

"Okay, give me a sec..." She was tapping keys. "It seems there's a tenant living there, a... Sorry, do you also live at the address?"

"No, I'm not calling about the house itself."

"Right..."

Scott sighed. He had to get it over with. "Apparently you saw my wife with another man."

"I don't understand," Rachel said.

Scott explained. He told her about finding Natalie's name on the wall and how cagey the tenant had been when Scott asked about it. "She said you made a joke. She implied it was about my wife and her lover."

Lover. Scott's hand was burning again. He hadn't replaced the cream all day.

"I wouldn't joke about our clients–"

"I don't think they were your clients–"

"Or *potential* clients. Or anybody."

Scott paused. Accusing her probably wasn't the best idea.

"Forget the joke. I must've got that part wrong. But did you see her, my wife?"

"I'm afraid I can't discuss that."

Scott's phone buzzed. A text appeared on the screen. It was Casey.

Don't take too long, honey. I miss you xxxxx

"You *can* discuss it with me." He slammed his good hand against the steering wheel. "My wife died by suicide and I think this man might know something about it. Please, you're my only chance."

That wasn't a lie. Perhaps the owner of the scraped-out name *did* know something. For what felt like the hundredth time, Scott cursed himself for not looking into this sooner. It had been so easy to ignore with Casey's smile, Casey's touch, Casey's everything to distract him.

"I saw your wife a few times." Rachel lowered her voice. "I'm sorry she passed. I didn't know that. But I'm not sure it's my place to tell you this."

"Tell me what?"

"I don't think–"

"Tell me *what?*"

After a pause, she went on. "Your wife would visit the park fairly often, at least while I was working around there. I'd see them both in the park, or near the entrance. Some nights, it would be just the two of them. In the park, I mean, no one else there."

"What would they do?"

"Just walk, from what I saw. Hold hands. Nothing much, really."

Scott stared out the window for a moment, looking at nothing. He was trying to picture Natalie holding somebody else's hand, the same way they'd held hands; he was trying to imagine her loving somebody else. Scott had felt physically incapable of feeling love for another person while he was with Natalie. Nobody else could compare, ever.

"Hello?" Rachel said.

"I'm here."

"Are you sure you want to know everything?"

"Yes," Scott said, though he *wasn't* sure.

"Well... your wife, the person she was with. I'm sorry. It was a woman."

"Oh." Scott slumped back, struggling to accept what he'd just heard. "A woman."

"Yes."

"I didn't... I never... I had no idea."

"Well." Her voice was tight. "You see why this wasn't really my place."

Scott stared down at his hands, at the bandaged hand and the one with half a pinkie finger. He studied his wedding ring, as he often found himself doing, but now he was thinking about his old ring: the one Natalie had slid onto his finger.

He remembered the shiny happiness in her eyes, the love. And she was hiding it, this, all along. He thought he'd known her completely; despite the pain it brought, the arguments, they'd been their true selves with each other.

"Her parents are religious. Properly religious. I wonder if

that's why she never said anything. Can you tell me what this other woman looked like? She might know something."

"I never saw her up close. I'm sorry."

"What about the details of the renters from around that time? Maybe they got a closer look at her."

"I can't–"

"Please. You don't know how badly I need this."

"I've said too much already."

She hung up. Scott thought about ringing back, but what would be the point? She'd only do the same. Plus he didn't know if he had another conversation in him.

His wife had been having an affair with a woman.

There had never been any signs, had there? Scott thought back, but all he could recall was the love, the closeness, the jokes and the warmth. If he wanted, there was more, ugly smears with which he might've marked their marriage. But he couldn't, not ever, and especially not after the car, unseeing eyes...

Nobody was perfect, not him, not Natalie.

Scott clearly hadn't paid very close attention. She'd been living a second life and he'd never guessed a thing.

No more sleepwalking through life. He was going to take control.

His phone buzzed again.

Tick-tock. You don't want to keep me waiting xxxxx

15

NATALIE

L *iving a lie.*
I'd never liked that phrase. It implied my entire existence was false, that there was nothing true about my life whatsoever. But that wasn't the case.

I enjoyed my time with my friends. I liked visiting Mum and Dad, even if I knew they'd never want to see me again if I told them the truth; they were evil when it came to gay people, truly evil, and yet I loved them too much to hate them for it.

I enjoyed reading and my hobbies and writing and all the rest of it.

But yes, when it came to my sexuality, I never told anybody... well, *almost* anybody.

I wasn't ashamed of being gay. It was Mum and Dad, knowing they'd never be able to accept me. So maybe that is a kind of shame. Whatever; I stowed it away, locked it in a corner of my mind, and tried to ignore it.

Scott often complained I didn't initiate sex enough. I knew it was difficult for him. He didn't understand why I wasn't like other women: why I was content to go weeks or even months without so much as a quickie. Sex with men simply didn't interest me. It never had. There was nothing personal about it. I could never remember being attracted to a man, or a boy when I was a child; it had been girls from the start.

But it wasn't just *me*. I can't take all the blame. Scott had his problems when it came to sex.

He'd often get rough without asking me first. We'd be making love – if I can call it that – with him on top. And then he'd suddenly grab me and flip me over, almost forcing me to my hands and knees. I'd go along with it, hoping it would be over soon. One time, after he'd put me in his preferred position, he began to spank me.

It was light at first, little playful taps. I wasn't into that sort of thing. But fine, I thought, if it helped him finish sooner... But then the spanks got harder, rougher, until he was basically punching my ass over and over. Pain bit into my back, up my spine, as some of his strikes missed. At least, I hoped he was doing it by mistake.

I moved away, crawling across the bed. "That's enough. I don't like it like that. You know I don't."

He stood at the end of the bed, his fists clenched, his cock still hard. My body froze when I saw the end of his dick was flecked in blood. I looked down, at the sheets, and saw ugly petals of it speckled all over the place. "How long have I been bleeding?"

Scott laughed in the nastiest way. "Fuck me, Nat. It's all about you. That was just getting good."

"Scott, I'm bleeding!"

He groaned. "You already said that. Right, what are we doing?"

"Maybe you could apologise."

"Are we finishing this or what? You're being so selfish right now."

"And you're being a pig."

"Fine, fuck off then." He walked over to the desk, grabbing the laptop and carrying it to the bed.

"What are you doing?"

"What does it look like? I'm not letting you spoil this. It's not like it makes much difference anyway. We only have sex once a year, if that."

"Scott." Despite how often he became like this, I began to cry. "That isn't true."

"Whatever."

He quickly typed on the laptop, bringing up a porn site. A second later, the most sickening video appeared on the screen. A girl who looked like a teenager was bent over in the middle of a dungeon, with countless men surrounding her, all of them exposed, all of them hard, as the girl moaned in what – to me – sounded like a completely fake way. Scott pumped his hand up and down his length, ignoring me, not even caring that I was watching the grotesque show.

I grabbed the blanket and wrapped it around myself, walking into the hallway, as the poor girl whined and screamed from the next room.

16

SCOTT

Scott looked forward to taking a dump these days. It almost made him laugh, as he sat there with his jeans around his ankles, staring at the bathroom door. Whenever he was home, it was only a matter of time before Casey decided to turn her attention to him. It had been three days since the conversation with the estate agent.

Casey's *games* had only gotten worse: forcing Scott to burn his belly with matches, making him watch as she set fire to photos of Natalie... That one had hurt, but Casey refused to believe him. "Are you really going to pretend this makes you *sad*? Oh, Scottie, you should've been an actor."

The previous night, she'd timed him as he completed a puzzle. It was a large one, with hundreds of pieces, a giant watercolour of a docked warship. She'd held her phone in her hand and a stopwatch in the other, grinning, tapping her newly manicured fingernail against her phone.

"I wonder who would be more shocked, the head or Natalie's parents."

Scott had never once completed a puzzle, but he found a way with the extra motivation. Somehow the image began to reveal itself, piece by piece, and this was how bad things had become; he was jealous of the damn puzzle. He wished Casey had revealed her true self a little bit at a time, instead of suddenly appearing, springing sadistically into existence.

Pieces, he could handle them, like teeth swilling around a blood-soaked mouth.

"One minute and twenty-two seconds left." Casey had laughed. "I wonder if you'll be as lucky next time."

Scott returned to the present when he heard her footsteps on the stairs. She paused outside the door. "Is there a problem in there?"

If Scott was superstitious, he would've said Casey had cast a spell on him. Every time she spoke his burnt hand throbbed. "I'm fine."

"You're taking a very long time. Are you sure you're not ill?"

He was taking a long time because it was his only chance to get away from her. "I'm fine."

"I'm fine, I'm fine," she mimicked. "B-O-R-I-N-G. Do you know what that spells?"

Scott wasn't sure how he was supposed to make having a shit interesting. He couldn't risk *not* answering. "It spells boring."

"At least you can do something right."

She left him. Scott hurried up, finishing his business.

As he left the bathroom, he passed evidence of his father's wasted inheritance money; there were new paintings on the walls, in expensive-looking frames, cardboard boxes scattered all over the place which had contained hair dryers and straighteners and a new vanity unit and countless other unnecessary items. So far, Casey had forced him to transfer nine thousand pounds, meaning he had sixty-three left in his savings account.

She was in the living room, staring at their new TV. "It has all the bells and whistles," she had proudly told him as the delivery drivers carried it in. "Thank you, you lovely boys." Casey had given them a large tip, fifty pounds each; the men had exchanged a glance and then quickly taken the money, smiling all the way back to their truck.

"How much, Casey?" Scott asked.

His heart was pounding at the base of his throat, the way it did any time he thought about challenging her. But this couldn't go on forever.

You're never going to let me go, are you?

"Sorry, sweetie?" Casey said.

Scott cringed. He hated when she talked to him like this, in a borderline loving way. It was too *old Casey.* "How much?"

Their new TV was a smart one; Casey picked up the remote and paused the programme. She turned slowly. She was purposefully taking her time. She was such a dramatic bitch. "How much for what?"

"For this to stop. Name a price."

"Are we negotiating?"

"I'm trying to."

"How funny." She furrowed her eyebrows. "Because here I was, under the impression I held all the cards. How silly of me. Okay then. Show me what you've got."

Scott was lost.

"No?" Casey sprung to her feet. She was wearing a new silk bathrobe; it looked too fancy to call a *dressing gown.* It fit her curvy form snugly. Scott hated his body's response, even now, betraying him at every turn. Casey knew the power she held over him, not just the phone, not just the violence. She moved her hips side to side as she approached. "Then it seems you've made a mistake, my darling husband. If you have nothing to bargain with, all you've done is ruin my good mood."

She walked past him, down the hallway, out the front door.

Scott went to the window and stared as she walked down the stone path to the gate. She unlocked it and pulled it open, wedging it in place with a garden ornament.

"The gate's open," she said when she returned. "I think you better go and close it."

Scott shrugged. As games went, this was far tamer than her usual tastes. "Fine."

"Nah-uh." She tittered. "Naked."

Scott paused at the door.

"Naked," she repeated sharply. "And consider yourself lucky that's all you're getting. Silly, silly Scott. As if there's a number that could make this go away. You know what you did. You know what you are."

She'd said similar things before. Scott had no idea what she was talking about. He wasn't without fault. Maybe he was a little absent-minded. Maybe he'd lost his temper a few times in his life, but nothing serious, nothing that would warrant this.

Nothing Casey could possibly know about.

"What if the neighbours see?"

It was almost five on a weekday, a bright late afternoon. Their garden was bordered by a fence. But that didn't mean somebody in an upper window might not happen to look out, to spot him. Or the neighbours across the street. Or a pedestrian.

"Don't make me ask again. I thought you were learning."

When she reached for her phone, Scott began to strip. His hands snapped to action far too eagerly, unbuttoning his shirt, slowly at first, but he needed to get this over with. He tore his clothes off, all of them, until he was standing naked in the hallway.

"Cold, is it?" Casey giggled.

He wanted to curse at her. He didn't.

He cracked the front door and peered outside.

Suddenly Casey pushed him. Scott stumbled and almost

tripped on the step, caught himself, her laughter ringing in his ears as he jogged for the gate. He slammed it shut and ran back down the path, thinking she might've closed and locked the door behind him.

But she was too busy: leaning against the wall, hands on her sides, laughing so hard her whole face and neck had turned red.

"You did it. You actually did it. You're even more pathetic than I thought."

Scott stood over her. He'd never fantasised so vividly about hitting anybody, especially not a woman. But he did then. He thought about the feeling of her cheekbone against his fist. The way her head would crack against the corner of the heater. The blood pooling.

She saw his look, stopped laughing. "Go on, big man. Show me who you really are."

Scott turned away and gathered up his clothes.

17

LAUREN

Lauren walked towards the library, wrapping her coat around herself. The wind was whipping along the waterfront that evening. She'd walked this same way so many times over the years, having been born in Bristol, ever since she was a little girl and her dad would take her on day-long sightseeing tours.

His favourite piece of history was always the SS *Great Britain*; they'd visited it countless times, and Lauren never got bored. It was the passion in her father's face, his voice. It was his curiosity, always eager to learn any new fact. It had ignited the same in Lauren. He was the reason she'd become so obsessed with history.

She was curious about everything, though, not just history; she read as much as she could and often watched documentaries. Mostly, she was fascinated by people. Scott's predicament was the *most* fascinating. She wouldn't phrase it that way to him. He was getting worse every day, the bags under his eyes getting deeper, darker.

But she was keen to get involved. There was no denying it.

Scott had said most people would run away from a problem like this. Lauren didn't care what most people did.

Scott had given her the details for the book club. As luck would have it, their next meeting was that week. Lauren had speed-read their thriller, finding it quite absorbing and interesting. But she wasn't attending to talk about the book.

Entering the library, she spotted the other women in the corner, sitting around a large table. Lauren recognised them from the Facebook discussion group.

The self-appointed queen bee was Izzy, an older woman with dyed pink hair and a staggering number of piercings, colourful tattoos covering her arms. Then there was Olivia, who looked every bit the librarian she was, with her mousy ponytail and her overbite and her big brown glasses.

Finally there was Fiona, the closest to Lauren's age. She had recently gone through a divorce; her Facebook wall was plastered with memes and statuses about it. She wore a chic poncho, her hair recently styled, as though she was screaming, *Screw you, world, I don't need a husband.*

"Lauren." Izzy rushed forwards, taking Lauren's hand, shaking it hard. Lauren smiled as she wondered if her shoulder would dislocate. "It's so nice to meet you in person."

"Thank you for having me. I know it was short notice. Am I late?"

"We're just getting started. You know Fiona and Olivia from Facebook, right? Right, let's get on with it."

Lauren sat and took the book from her handbag. She'd ordered it for next-day delivery, but the other three had Kindles.

"A purist, I see," Izzy joked.

Lauren chuckled. "Guilty as charged."

"I used to be," Olivia said. "As a librarian, I considered it my *duty*. But my eyes... you can't change font size in a paperback."

"I consider all kinds of reading valid," Lauren said.

"Ah, a politician," Izzy replied.

"Hardly. I wish I made as much as one though."

Lauren waited to see if they'd take the bait. She had a plan. She wasn't sure if it was a good one, but she wanted to try; anyway, she was feeling impatient.

"Unfortunately, teaching assistants don't get the same benefits as MPs."

"Where to do you teach?" Fiona asked.

Lauren gave the name of the school, watching for their reactions. There was something: a general tightening of their expressions. "I like it," she went on. "I feel lucky to be able to work most days. A lot of people are with agencies, being carted from school to school. I mostly work with one teacher, history, which is a dream: the subject, not the teacher."

"What's his name?" Fiona said.

She seemed like the most interested, staring at Lauren as though starved for gossip.

"Scott," Lauren said.

"Scott..."

"Smith." Lauren shrugged, feigning confusion when Fiona's eyebrows shot up. "I feel like I'm missing something."

"*He* was the one who missed something." Fiona's words rushed out. "He missed the chance to mourn for his wife. He missed the chance to be a good husband. Natalie was so... and he just moved on, but that's men, that's men. My own was the same. Cheating bastard. I bet Scott was cheating too. I bet he was with Casey before she– Poor girl, poor Natalie. I wish she'd spoken to us..."

It was like she was trying to break the world record for speaking quickly. Lauren had to concentrate so she didn't miss anything. "I don't understand."

"There's some history there," Olivia said quietly.

"Yes, there is." Izzy glared at Fiona. "But I don't think it's our place to say."

"I bet Scott's regretting his decision now." Fiona laughed darkly.

"Wait a second." Lauren was playing the ditsy blonde, all wide-eyed and confused. "Are you telling me you know Scott?"

"We knew his wife. *Both* his wives." Fiona frowned. "God, I still can't believe they got married."

"You said he regretted it," Lauren murmured. "He seems pretty happy to me."

"Give it time. Just ask her last–"

"All right, class, gossiping time's over." Izzy laughed, but there was an edge to it. "I've been looking forward to this all month. Let's not ruin it with that rubbish. Shall we get started?"

Lauren wanted to push harder, but Olivia and Izzy were ready to move on; Fiona went with the flow, though Lauren could tell she was willing to say more. But that was fine, enough for that evening. She had her target. Fiona was going to tell her everything she needed to know.

As they discussed the book, Lauren thought about what Fiona had said.

Just ask her last–

Her last what? Her last husband? Her last victim?

Whatever it was, Lauren would find out.

She wouldn't waste this chance.

18

SCOTT

"I can't believe it," Gary said, for what seemed like the fifteenth time.

They were sitting in the pub, in their usual spot. Scott's hand throbbed when he picked up his pint to take a sip. He had to make sure not to drink too much; Casey had sternly warned him not to be drunk when he came home. He placed the glass down carefully. Scott could've used his other hand, the unbandaged one, but in a sick way he savoured the pain.

"Scott?"

"Neither can I," he said after a pause.

"You had no idea she was gay?"

Scott shook his head. "I thought we were happy. I thought we were in love. I didn't know she had a second life."

Gary sat back. "Have you thought about the obvious yet?"

"Yeah. Casey and Natalie were together. Casey got angry when Natalie killed herself. She blamed me. And here we are. It's possible, isn't it?"

"It is. You think Lauren will come through with the book club?"

Scott shrugged. "I was shocked she even offered. I feel like I don't know a bloody thing anymore."

"Are things *that* bad?"

Scott moved his finger around the rim of his glass, his mind flashing alight with Casey's face as she tortured him. There had been more *games* since she'd forced him to walk naked to the garden gate; he hated thinking about them and had no desire to relive them. "Yeah. I had to beg for permission to come here. I think she knows something's going on, but she's too arrogant to care. She knows she's got me by the balls."

"Jesus."

"She searches me at random times too. Just in case I try to record her. If I ever *do* try–"

"She releases the videos."

I will make you bleed, you little bitch.

"Exactly," Scott said, hating the voice. The memory.

"Christ."

They drank quietly for a time. A family was laughing a few tables over, the daughter's giggle ringing out above it all. Scott found himself wondering when Natalie had known she liked women. Had she been older than that girl? She must've been so scared of her parents, listening to them talk about how evil it was, how hotly the sinners would burn.

So that was that, then: no religion for Scott. He'd passed several churches on the way to the pub, entertained – briefly – the notion of going inside one of them.

"She let the timer run down to a minute last night. On the draft. She was grinning at me in that freaky way, holding her finger over the *edit draft* button. She loves watching me squirm. Maybe I should just let her release it."

"Seriously? That would mean the end of your career."

"I know."

"You love being a teacher."

"I know that too."

"You're not acting like you know. You're acting like you've already given up."

"Maybe I'm not as strong as you think I am. Maybe I never have been."

"That's bullshit. We can do this. We can find a way to fight back."

"No offence, but I don't feel like *we're* doing anything. I'm the one who's turned into her personal plaything. I'm the one who has to put up with her..." Scott had sat up, his words booming through the pub. The family had stopped laughing; they were staring at him. He slumped back in his chair. "Sorry. I don't know where that came from."

"You don't have to apologise."

They sat quietly for a time, making progress on their drinks. Scott glanced at the clock above the bar. He had twenty minutes before he needed to begin the drive home. Anything could be waiting for him when he opened the door.

"I've got a confession to make," Gary said.

"Yeah?"

"I rang that estate agent pretending to be a police officer."

"Are you serious?"

"Yeah. After you told me what she said – Rachel – I knew I had to help. We need to know who lived in that house before. Maybe they'll recognise Natalie's..."

"Girlfriend. It's all right. You can say it."

Gary went on. "I rang them up and said I was looking into some burglaries from around that time. It was all crap, obviously. But she didn't know any better. I've got the address and phone number of the previous tenant. Her name is Tess Foster. Luckily she's still with the same estate agent, so Rachel was able to give it to me."

"You could get in trouble for that," Scott said. "I don't want to ruin your life as well."

Gary shook his head. "After everything you've done for me, you think I'm going to make you go through this alone?"

"Mate–"

"I'd be dead if it wasn't for you. Do you want the details or not?"

Scott thought of the blood and the screaming and all that youthful fire in his chest, and, like the fool he was, he'd truly believed it would never stop burning. He was only thirty-six, but sometimes he felt ancient.

"Of course I bloody do."

Gary reached into his jacket pocket and brought out a piece of paper, sliding it across the table.

This Tess Foster had a life of her own, friends and family; she didn't want to be involved in Scott's hell.

But he couldn't ignore this chance. Maybe she'd be able to tell him if Casey had been the other woman. That, at least, would make sense. It would give Casey a motive to do this. People had whispered after Natalie's death. Nobody had outright accused him of murder, but when a wife killed herself, the husband was the most natural candidate to blame.

It would be even easier for Natalie's girlfriend – always on the sidelines, hating Scott – to come to that conclusion.

He should've done more. He should've known her better. He should've paid closer attention.

It didn't help that it was all true. He *should* have done all those things.

Scott took out his phone, dialling the number.

"You're ringing her now?" Gary said.

Scott looked at the clock again. "Yeah."

Minutes were ticking by; he needed hope, if he was going to endure whatever was waiting for him that evening.

19

SCOTT

"Hello?" The woman sounded nervous, as though she wasn't used to receiving phone calls.

"Hello, am I speaking with Tess Foster?"

"Who is this?"

Gary was staring at him wide-eyed, eager. Despite everything, Scott could tell there was a tiny glimmer of fun in this for his friend. Gary had a nine-to-five and two children. He had a mortgage and two cars on finance and he listened to podcasts on the way to work; he had a regular life, so this must've been an interesting break from it, at the very least.

"My name is Scott Smith. This is going to seem a little strange, but I think you may know something about my wife. I think you may have seen her from your old house, the one that overlooked the park. She was with another woman."

"Ah."

Gary gave Scott a look, a question in his raised eyebrow. Scott shook his head. Maybe. They were getting there.

"Her name was Natalie–"

"I never knew their names."

Scott's heart beat a little faster. "But you saw them?"

"I did more than see them, young man."

Scott found himself grinning. He was often noticing his smiles lately. They felt unusual. "Who said I was young?"

"Your voice. Go on, guess how old I am. It's a game I like to play."

"Twenty-six."

She laughed, and Scott smiled again. "Not even close. I've just turned eighty, in fact."

"Happy birthday."

"Thank you. That's very kind of you to say."

Scott warned himself not to hope too strongly. But there was no denying this was the best person they could've found. She was old, possibly lonely, and seemed keen to talk.

"Natalie... She was the one with black hair, straightened if she wore it down, in a ponytail if not. She was tall, and on the thin side."

"Yes, she sounds familiar."

"What did you see?" Scott asked. "Did you see them together?"

"Her and her girlfriend, yes, yes I did. But I must say, I'm not in the habit of helping husbands snoop on their wives."

"She's dead. And whatever you tell me will be strictly between us." Scott couldn't afford to be honest. "How often did you see them?"

"Dead? That's awful. How, if you don't mind me asking?"

"Suicide. I found her. She mentioned the park in her note, which is why I'm calling."

"Goodness gracious." When she paused, Scott imagined her making the sign of the cross. "When did this happen?"

"Almost two years ago."

"And you're only *just* looking into this?"

Scott's grip tightened on the phone. He didn't need her to remind him of what an idiot he'd been. Maybe he could forgive himself for the first few months, when it had been an effort to get out of bed, to shower, to brush his teeth: when the grief had swallowed him up. But what about after?

"Life got in the way. Please."

Tess sighed. "I'm not sure I should tell you this..."

"You said you'd done more than see them." Scott felt like he was chasing a bone. "What did you mean?"

"It was a horrible thing. She cursed at me. She told me to never tell anybody what I'd seen."

"Who cursed at you? Natalie? The one with the black hair? The tall one?"

"I can't remember," she snapped. "One of them. I know that much. One of them shouted at me and I thought it was *very* unnecessary. I have every right to walk down my own street."

This had happened years ago. It made sense that she wouldn't remember all the specifics, but Scott felt like she was holding something back.

"What happened?"

"And this is between us, yes? Just us?"

"Yes."

Another lie. Scott would use whatever ammunition he could get his hands on. He'd fire it right down Casey's throat to make her back off. He'd choke the bitch.

Of course you will, big man. You can do anything.

"I'd seen them many times in the park," Tess went on. "They'd walk hand in hand under the trees. They'd often linger near the hangman's tree, kissing, holding each other. I thought it was quite romantic, truthfully. To see love like that... I'm sorry, I never knew she was married."

"It's fine." Scott's throat was tight as he thought about all the times Natalie had turned away from a kiss, told him she was too tired, said she wasn't in the mood. She needed her space. She was stressed at work. But she'd been saving it for somebody else. So many arguments made sense now. "So they looked like they were in love…"

"They *were* in love," Tess said. "I was with my Alfred for fifty-two years. I know love when I see it. I had no ill will towards them whatsoever. That's what made it so shocking."

Scott waited. In the background, a cat meowed, then another. He imagined her sitting in a rocking chair, by the window, peering out onto the street as dozens of cats lazed around her.

"I'd run out of milk, so naturally I left to get some. On my way home – it was late, perhaps almost half past nine, and it was dark – I happened to see them at the end of the street, near the entrance to the park. They spotted me. And then one of them came marching across the street. She screamed at me, waving her finger in my face, telling me to mind my own business. I only had a little look. That was all. It was rather uncalled for, in my view."

"Do you think you'd recognise them, if I showed you photos? I could send you some right now."

Scott couldn't imagine Natalie screaming at a stranger. She never snapped like that in public. But Casey was a drugged-up lunatic; she was making no effort to hide her use. He could imagine her behaving in that way.

"I don't have a computer."

"I can send it to your phone."

"Oh, I don't want to mess around with that nonsense."

"I can come to you with photos."

"To my house?" Her voice trembled. "I don't think that would be very appropriate. How did you get this number? I never asked, did I? Did I ask?"

Scott swallowed. "Yeah, you did. And I told you I'd gotten it from the estate agent."

"Oh."

She sounded so horribly confused. Scott thought of his grandfather, who'd suffered with dementia at the end; he felt like dirt. "Maybe I could visit you one day. We could have tea. I'll even bring some biscuits."

"No– I don't think– No, no thank you. Goodbye."

She hung up.

"So, what did she say?" Gary asked.

Scott told him everything. "I think I scared her when I said I was going to visit her. But I need to know. Maybe she'll recognise a photo of Natalie, of Casey... if the other woman is Casey. I'll just need to figure out a time to go."

"I could go," Gary said.

Scott shrugged. "It might come to that. But I'd like to, if I can get a chance. I want to see for myself if she recognises either of them. Can you imagine Natalie flying off the handle like that?"

"No."

"Me neither."

Not at an innocent old lady.

Scott's phone buzzed. He grabbed it, read the text.

I need another 5k, darling. There's a dress on sale and I MUST have it xxxxx

"I take it that's not good?"

Scott laughed darkly. He was down to fifty-one thousand. She was bleeding his inheritance away on fancy ballgowns she was never going to wear, TVs she rarely watched, exercise equipment she hadn't even unpacked yet. She rarely looked at the things she'd bought when they arrived, only at Scott, as if savouring every little moment.

"At least we made some progress." Scott navigated to his banking app, arranging the payment. "Maybe this will all be over soon."

Gary stared down into the dregs of his pint, then looked up at Scott, his expression grim. "Yeah, maybe."

20

CASEY

Casey took a sip of wine and tucked her legs up beneath herself, browsing the websites on her phone. She had fifteen tabs open: make-up and clothes and holidays and vintage cheese knives and bespoke saunas, delivery included...

With a simple tap of her finger, *poof*, more of Scottie's money disappeared. She was a little surprised he hadn't refused to transfer the funds yet, but she'd underestimated how narcissistic he was.

His image was all that mattered. The teacher who did his best by his students; the mostly kind man who sometimes made mistakes, like marrying a woman too soon after his wife's death. The naïve boyish bloke who, nonetheless, had good intentions in his heart.

But that was a lie. Scott's heart was broken and corrupted. *I want to tell you a story about a handsome king and his princess, and a love the world could never understand...*

Casey finished off her wine in a violent gulp, looking at the clock.

Scott had eleven minutes left. She doubted he'd be late. So far, he'd submitted to everything she'd demanded. He was willing to make a fool of himself, even to physically harm himself to stop the world from seeing him with his hand wrapped around his worm.

She navigated to her photos, skipping past the familiar ones – the ones she'd shown Scott – and selecting the newer ones.

Her body glowed, a ball expanding from deep inside, starlight and goodness and pleasure tickling every part of her.

Scott crawled around on the floor, nuzzling the carpet, making purring noises as he tried to reach the treat at the end of the piece of string. *He is the weak one, the little puny one, the dead-headed one.* Casey was off-camera, pulling the treat away, as Scott meowed and licked his lips. He'd begged her not to do this, but it was too hilarious.

The next one had Casey giggling like crazy.

Scott was tied to a chair, his hands behind his back, completely naked. Casey was behind him, ducked down so the camera couldn't see her face; her arm snaked around and she took him in her hand, stroking aggressively, hard, making him feel it, *really* feel it. She'd only been able to study his face afterward, on video, revelling in the twisted transformation.

First he was angry, all demon-eyed, but then his instincts started to kick in. He couldn't help it. Casey had replayed one part many times: the moment Scott realised he was beginning to enjoy it. His eyes widened like a cartoon character, and then his lips made a weird shape, not quite a grimace, not quite a smile. "Please, please."

Even *he* didn't know if he was begging her to stop or keep going. Towards the end, Casey had moaned for him, driving him closer and closer. And then, once he'd spilled his feeble little load, Casey had smoothed her hand up his belly. She'd gathered it all up – thinking that surely this was it; surely he'd draw the line here – and brought her hand to his mouth.

Too quiet for the camera, she'd whispered, "Drink it, Scottie. You know you want to."

And he *had*.

She moved her hands over her belly, laughing so hard it hurt. It was all there in his face: his need to be strong, to be in charge, to put Casey in her place. But he couldn't. He was a weasel.

There were more, but that one was hard to top. She'd made him eat several bowlfuls of spinach, which he hated. He'd vomited at the end. There were a couple of them having sex, which Casey would never show anybody; she had never enjoyed their sex before, but it was different now.

Casey placed her phone down and climbed to her feet. She wanted to unpack Scott's present before he got home.

21

SCOTT

Scott paused at the gate, squeezing onto the cold metal. It hadn't even been two weeks since Casey revealed her true nature. It felt like much longer, like he'd become a completely different person. Every thought roared at him to get away from here, to get away from *her*.

She was going to play her sick games. She was going to force him to have sex with her. She might even make him burn himself again, or worse.

He never knew what was waiting for him.

As he walked up the path, he thought about what he'd mentioned to Gary. He could get out of this situation any time he wanted. All he had to do was call her bluff: let her release the photos and the videos. No parent would ever want him around their kids again, but he'd still have fifty grand in savings; he'd still have a life worth living.

Wouldn't he?

What if Casey never stopped?

Even if Scott moved away to start a new life, she'd find him. She'd show the videos to everybody. Even if people might pretend not to care, it changed a person, being publicly exposed like that. He'd always have it dangling over his head. He'd always feel different, separate from everybody else, dirty.

This was the argument he had with himself every time he walked up the path. Lately, he was starting to wonder if the truth was much simpler. He was scared. Not of the videos, not of the photos, not of the blackmail. He was scared of his wife.

The things she did, the things she made him do, she smiled, she laughed, she revelled in it. There was never any doubt or regret or moment of pause. After, she often stared at him like it was his fault the fun had stopped: like her toy was malfunctioning.

That was the look. The terror in it.

She was getting bored. She was going to escalate things.

Casey was waiting for him in the hall. Scott hated how beautiful she looked in her silk night-robe: one of half a dozen she now owned. He hated her hair, its messy sexiness, her flushed cheeks. He hated her full and tempting thighs. He hated himself for still finding her attractive, on a physical level, when he should've known better. When he *did* know better. It was only certain parts that forgot how evil she was.

She gestured to an object at her feet.

It was a large dog cage, the door open. She'd put Scott's pillow in there. Casey had lovingly teased him when he bought it a few months ago; it was memory foam and was supposed to help with neck ache.

"You're so silly," she'd said, her voice airy, her voice *hers*: the Casey he'd known for over a year, the woman he kept expecting to snap back into existence any moment.

"I bought you a new bed, honey." Now *this* Casey smiled. "What's wrong? Don't you like it?"

You're a pathetic bitch. You fucking mess. I'm going to hurt you. Badly. Both fists were clenched as he remembered old fights, as he remembered swinging his fists with his teeth gritted and adrenaline rushing into his head; it made him think of his father, and he suddenly envied him. That freedom to rage. It was a horrible thought.

Scott bowed his head. "Yes, I like it. Thank you."

It was awkward, climbing into the cage. He tried not to look at her. The quality of her breathing had changed. It got quicker when she was humiliating him, panting.

His back was already aching as he hunched over.

She left the room and returned with a padlock. "There we go, safe and sound."

She locked it with a heavy *click*.

22

NATALIE

Scott got a sick thrill from making me sleep in a dog cage. This was after the yelling, the holes he'd punched into the walls, after he'd pressured me into having sex more times than I could count. This was after the broken promises; it was after he'd made me so scared of him, sometimes I couldn't sleep, lying awake, grateful for the hours of darkness and silence.

He didn't hit me. That was his only redeeming quality, if such a basic thing as *do not hit your wife* can be considered a positive characteristic.

The first time he showed me the dog cage, I told him no. I thought he was joking. Our marriage was confused like that; amidst all the shouting and the arguing, there was love, there was respect sometimes. There was something real.

His breath reeked of whisky as he moved closer. "I'm not messing around, you stupid slut. You're sleeping in there tonight."

"Scott–"

"If you don't..." He got even closer. "I'll tell your backward parents you cheated on me. Can you imagine their faces?

They'd soak their Bibles with all their crying. They'd disown you."

I froze. For a second I thought he knew about the affair, knew about *her*. But he didn't. It was all part of the threat; he was saying he was going to lie to them about a fake affair. He didn't know about the real one.

"Why, Scott?" I whispered.

"Why?" He laughed, making it sound violent, like a jagged cough. "*Why*? You know why."

He stared for a second, and then it hit me. The other night, I'd been performing oral sex on him. And then he'd become aggressive, pushing far too deep. I'd started to choke and he'd grabbed my hair, and then, when I pushed against his legs to make him stop, he'd taken it as a sign that I was enjoying it. Or he'd pretended to.

I'd finally managed to get away from him. He'd become pouty, as he had many times before. "You always ruin it when it's getting good."

"It's your choice," he said. "The cage or I ring the religious nutjobs. What's it going to be?"

Scott knew how much my parents mattered to me. He knew how much I loved them. Any sort of scandal would ruin them; whenever anything happened in their lives, their first question was always how their church friends would react to it. It was always how things *seemed*, rather than what they were. Scott knew I couldn't bear to inflict that on them. Even if they maybe deserved it.

As I climbed into the cage, he stood with his legs apart, one hand casually stroking up and down his crotch.

23

SCOTT

Scott tried to get into a comfortable position. His legs were squashed sideways and there was nowhere to rest his head. The best he could do was draw his knees to his chest and wrap his arms around them, leaning back, his neck bent at an awkward angle.

He wasn't sure how much time had passed. Casey had spent the evening doing typically terrible things; she'd produced a BB gun, one Scott hadn't known she had, and shot him as he attempted to dodge within the confines of the cage. The pellets had been metal, ricocheting off the cage's bars with a loud clang... or slipping through the bars, pinging off his skin, leaving red marks.

They still pulsed, hours later.

After she'd grown tired of the BB gun, she'd left him in the hallway. The front door let in a draft and the heating was turned off. Scott shivered, wishing she'd given him a blanket at least.

He remembered what Gary said in the pub, about how much Scott loved teaching, about not giving up. But surely nothing was worth this. And yet Scott didn't call upstairs; he didn't tell Casey to release the videos and photos, to end it.

So apparently it *was* worth it. Or maybe this was just the sort of man he was. Ready or wanting to be beaten and controlled. Self-flagellating monks came to mind. He wasn't sure he'd be able to do that.

After a while – hours maybe – he needed to piss, but there was no way he was going to tell Casey. It was late. She was upstairs, perhaps sleeping or perhaps brainstorming new ways to hurt him. Several times Scott had to fight off tears, useless bloody tears, as his bladder ached and his shame grew.

What sort of man let this happen?

He almost laughed. A wilfully blind one. A gullible one.

Natalie, the love of his life, had been gay and he'd had no idea. Or, at the very least, she'd been bisexual. She was having an affair. He'd never suspected any of it. He went back through his memories, sorting like a picture book, looking for signs.

There was Natalie's reluctance to have sex. She'd always had a lower sex drive than him. Often they found workarounds when she wasn't in the mood; she'd use her hands, or pose for him on the bed as he took care of himself. He would ask her if *she* wanted anything, and she'd look at him in a confused way, as though the question was absurd.

What could she possibly want from her husband?

If he pressed, they'd get into an argument. Sometimes it would end in the ugliest way.

Plenty of wives weren't in the mood when their husbands wanted them to be. Scott had concluded it was work stress. Or maybe it was her writing course. She often worried about her assignments for days, weeks, where that class was concerned; she'd rant and fall into a depression. "I'm never going to make it. The odds are stacked against me."

"You will," he'd tell her, pulling her into his arms, kissing the top of her head. "I believe in you."

"I don't say this enough, but you really are the best husband."

That made it all better: the arguments and the pain. The tenderness, the love, *that* was their marriage. Not the rest of it.

Other than the sex, Scott couldn't think of any indicators. He'd taken Natalie's detached nature as a symptom of her busy imagination. But truthfully she was somewhere else in her mind, with her lover, pretending Scott didn't exist.

He tilted his head from side to side, working out some of the tension in his neck. He wanted to hate Natalie. But he couldn't. Any time rage rose up, it was quickly followed by a vignette of how she'd looked in death, with her skin seeming somehow colourless, her eyes vacant, her stare full of nothing.

Scott wondered what had triggered the suicide. It clearly had something to do with her lover. She was thinking of her in the final moments: her, not Scott, not her parents.

Scott's bladder gave another pulse. He was trying to fight it. If one of his students whined they needed to the toilet on a school trip, he'd tell them to cross their legs and wait. Now he realised what a dick move that was.

He hoped Lauren had something for him soon. The teaching assistant was hard-working and had great attention to detail. People generally liked her. She'd be able to ingratiate herself into the book club, get the information Scott needed. *If* there was any information to be had.

All of this – investigating Natalie's suicide, digging into Casey's past – it could lead nowhere. It was all blind hope. It was all faith. He needed it.

More time passed. Scott's body tried to drag him down to sleep, but his need to piss jolted him awake each time. Dark and light, waking and sleeping, and then he woke with tears streaming hotly down his cheeks. He must've been dreaming, though he couldn't remember it.

Urine flooded his underwear, seeping down his thighs, pooling beneath him. It spread around the cage. He reeked. He buried his face in his hands, unable to stop, wishing this would end: wishing he had a way out that wouldn't blow his life up.

He wanted Natalie, his Nat, wanted her to hold him the same way she had after his father died. She'd embraced him so tightly, her fingers sinking into his back, so hard it was almost painful. But he didn't care. She was there; she was never going to leave him. Everything else had faded; he forgot they'd ever behaved cruelly to each other. There was only love.

"It's all going to be okay," he imagined her saying. "Just hold on a little longer."

He finally stopped pissing. Shifting to the other side of the cage – not that it was big enough to have much of *another side* – he moved as far away from the puddle of urine as he could. His boxers were soaked. He knew he should try to take them off, but standing was impossible. If he straightened his legs and shimmied out of his trousers, he'd end up spreading the piss everywhere.

He thought for a moment, and then pulled his T-shirt over his head, bumping his hands against the top of the cage. He'd mop it up with his T-shirt, push it through the bars of the cage, and then lie down and wriggle out of his trousers and take his underwear off.

A floorboard creaked upstairs.

Casey walked across the landing; he could hear her at the top of the stairs.

But then she passed, heading for the bathroom.

24

LAUREN

People were reckless when it came to social media. Lauren knew this wasn't a world-shattering observation, but it still baffled her.

Ever since the book club meeting, she'd been trying to think of a way to get some one-on-one time with Fiona; she'd easily been the biggest gossiper, the keenest to talk about Casey and her history in the book club. Lauren had a life, a partner, a flat, things to do, hobbies and interests, but this had niggled.

Scott's worsening condition hurried her along. Each day he came into work, he looked less like himself. The previous day he'd flinched when one of the students slammed their bag down on the table. He'd laughed afterwards, making a joke, but his voice had been shaking; his eyes had flitted over the classroom, as though expecting to find Casey.

Lauren wanted him to be okay. Even if she might have to hurt him one day. Either way, she wasn't going to stop. And if she found something, maybe she could use it. Maybe she'd do a little blackmailing of her own.

Fiona had a habit of checking in on Facebook. Lauren would never understand the desire.

Hello, world, just in case you wanted to know, I'm having a coffee at this precise location.

Lauren walked into the café. Fiona's check-in location was only a twenty-minute walk from her flat. Hopefully Fiona was still there.

Lauren wandered over to the counter, doing her best to seem natural as she looked around. It was late Friday afternoon, making it the two-week anniversary of Scott's dick pic. She grinned to herself as she thought about getting him a card. But she shouldn't smile; she didn't know if he was a bad person.

The café was busy, a stylish place, with a wooden ship's wheel mounted on the wall. A piano sat in the corner, and there were a bunch of knick-knacks along the windowsills.

Fiona was sitting in the corner, alone, with her Kindle on the table. Lauren got ready to do some acting. She'd never been much good in drama class.

"Fiona?"

Fiona looked up as Lauren walked over. Confusion registered on her face, then she smiled. "Lauren, right? Sorry. I'm terrible with names."

"Well, you got mine right."

"Phew." Fiona chuckled. "What are you doing here? I mean, obviously you're getting a coffee, but any particular reason?"

Fiona was speaking quickly, the same way she had at the book club. She seemed like a naturally anxious person.

"I'm stalking you. I followed you here."

Fiona laughed again and Lauren laughed along with her.

"Are you staying long?" Lauren asked. "This place is heaving..."

Fiona took the hint. "You can sit with me, if you want."

"Really? That's so nice. Let me repay you with a coffee. What's your poison?"

Fiona asked for a double espresso and Lauren ordered a

latte for herself. Fiona slugged the espresso back like it was a shot of whisky, then ran her hand through her hair: dyed and layered, with little beads and gems woven into it.

"What are you reading?" Lauren asked.

They made chit-chat for a while, talking about books. Lauren's chance came when Fiona asked about work.

"It's okay," she said. "I love my job. I'm grateful to have a steady teaching assistant gig. But my boss is being such a pain in the arse."

"Your boss, as in Scott?"

"Yeah. He's been so snappy lately, for no reason. I even called him out on it the other day."

"Oh?" Fiona was gazing hungrily, ready to devour every little gossipy morsel.

"I waited until after class and told him he couldn't shout at me in front of the students. It's unprofessional. I actually felt bad for him. He was so apologetic. He ended up telling me he was having problems at home."

Fiona laughed harshly. "What a surprise."

"Huh?"

"It's a miracle Scott and Casey have even lasted this long. I don't want to speak out of turn, but, well…"

The door to the café opened and a man walked in, shouting into his phone. Everybody glared at him, looked at each other to confirm their glaring was justified, and then returned to their private conversations, as his voice rose over the soft music playing on the speaker systems. "I don't *care* how long it takes. Just get it *done*."

Fiona rolled her eyes. "Some people are so clueless."

"I won't argue with that."

"What was I saying?" Fiona asked.

Lauren feigned confusion. She didn't want to seem too impatient. "Something about Casey?"

"That's right." Fiona grimaced. "Between you and me, I never liked her. She was always so fake. Everybody else loved her. Natalie really liked her, but then Natalie always enjoyed nasty jokes."

"Nasty jokes?"

"Casey had a twisted sense of humour. Most of the time, she was Miss Nice, you know the type, always remembering to ask about your family and this and that, but it just seemed so forced. It was like she'd read a book called *How to be a Human Being*. Nobody else seemed to notice. But sometimes, she'd let out her mean side. I remember this one time we were at a bar and there was this larger woman there, and Casey just kept going on and on about it, to the point the woman overheard and started to cry."

"And Natalie liked that?" Lauren asked, an edge to her voice.

"Natalie was laughing the hardest," Fiona said. "But she was drunk. We all were."

"Maybe that's it then." Lauren shrugged. "Maybe Casey's letting out her nasty side with Scott."

"I wouldn't be surprised, but don't mention I said anything, will you?"

"Of course not. I promise."

This was wrong, using her like this. Lauren was glad when Fiona smiled, seeming relieved.

Lauren sipped her coffee.

"You know," Fiona said a moment later. "The only time I ever saw Casey seem *not fake*, it was with her daughter–"

"Casey has a daughter?" Lauren cut in.

Fiona arched her eyebrow. "I thought you worked with Scott?"

"I do. He never mentioned Casey having a daughter."

"Yes, a daughter and an ex-husband. Poor man."

"Poor man? Why?"

Fiona looked around, as though making sure nobody was eavesdropping. "He came to the book club once. Livid. Apparently Casey had picked up their daughter from school and taken her to the cinema without his permission. He has full custody. Which is unusual, isn't it? We can say what we want, about how modern it is, but it's unusual for a man to have full custody. I'm not saying it's always the case. But I'm telling you. I saw how vicious she is. She was always putting me down, making me feel small."

Lauren's mind went to dark places, as she thought about a woman like Casey having a child, an innocent who'd never question her motives, who'd do whatever she asked.

"I'm sorry," Lauren said. "That's not okay."

"Thank you." Fiona smiled, a real *I'm making a new friend* smile, and Lauren felt like crap. "Anyway, Markus comes storming in, ready for a fight. Casey tried to play it cool at first, all nice, but then she snapped. She knocked my coffee over when she jumped to her feet. She was angrier than I'd ever seen anyone, I swear. She was screaming at him, calling him every name you can think of, C and P and F and all the rest of it."

"And then what happened?" Lauren asked.

"Markus grabbed Casey and whispered something in her ear. And then – like magic – she stopped. She calmed down. She collected her things and left, and that was that. It was weird."

Stopping Casey. Like magic. It sounded good. "What did he say?"

"No idea. It must've been something serious. Maybe he threatened to call the police. Whatever it was, it worked. Markus never came to the book club again. Casey must've behaved."

Lauren picked up her coffee, took a long sip. So that was her next step. The husband.

She was thinking about possible ammunition.

The question was, who would she use it against?

Scott or Casey?

"I didn't know she had an ex-husband," Scott said.

Lauren gawped at him from the other side of the desk. It was Monday lunchtime; the weekend had been predictably evil, especially when Casey discovered Scott had pissed himself in the cage. She'd loved that, giggling in that weird psycho way of hers. After that: more games, more so-called fun, more torture, more hate. Scott didn't let himself think about it at work.

You really are a coward.

"How is that even possible?" Lauren said.

And a fucking idiot.

Scott gripped his stress ball, squeezed, squeezed some more. "She lied. I asked if she'd ever been married, she said no, and that was good enough for me."

"But she knew Natalie. She was friends with her."

"So?" Scott snapped. "It's not like I know everything about my wife's friends."

"Did you know she has a daughter too?"

Scott dropped the ball and massaged his forehead. Lack of sleep was making him drink more and more coffee. The caffeine was making his head pulse. But it was the only way he could stay awake. "No."

"Scott, I'm sorry..."

"What?"

Lauren fiddled with her bracelet. "It's nothing."

"Just say it."

"Fine. Do you know your wife at *all*? I don't understand how you can be married to this person and have no idea of who they really are. Even Fiona – that's the woman from the book club – even she sensed something was off with Casey."

"She fucked me blind and she got me addicted to her body. She cooked dinner every night and never once asked me to do the dishes and never asked me to do any chores either. For months I was dead, Lauren, *dead* after Natalie's suicide. I felt like I was sleepwalking. And then Casey came along, and... and she brought me back to life."

"Okay, Scott. All right."

He realised he'd risen to his feet; he was staring down at Lauren. Lauren's expression was ridiculous. It was like she thought he was going to lash out at her.

"I'm sorry." He sat. "All of this, it's just..."

"I know."

But Lauren didn't sound like she'd accepted his apology. Her voice was tight. She was studying him closely, as she sat upright in her chair, as though ready to run away if he leapt at her.

Go on hit me hit me like the fucking big man you are.

"I'm sorry," he said.

"I've never seen you like that before."

"It's her, what's happening at home. It's like all this energy's bottled up, but I shouldn't have taken it out on you. It won't happen again."

"All right. That's fine. Yeah."

They paused for a time. Everything was making Scott want to snap. The children shouting outside the classroom, the dryness of his throat, the pulsing in his head. Even the tinkling sound Lauren's bracelet made as she endlessly fiddled with it.

"I accepted everything she told me," Scott said. "She didn't have social media. I couldn't find anything about her online. Not that I looked too hard. I was just glad to have somebody."

"I understand."

"I need to speak with her husband. He might be able to tell me something."

Lauren's expression softened. "I managed to find him on Facebook."

"How?"

"I had his first name and the fact he'd been married to Casey. There was an article online, celebrating their wedding. Her maiden name was mentioned."

He didn't miss the note at the end. "All right then, sue me. I never googled my fiancée. I ate up every last morsel of shit she fed me without second-guessing it. Happy?"

"It's fine."

"I've still got no bloody clue why you're doing this." Scott tightened his grip even more on the ball, holding it in his burned hand.

"Believe it or not, you grumpy dickhead, I actually quite like you. I'll text you the husband's Facebook page."

"No, just tell me. Don't text me anything."

Lauren looked at him for a moment. "She searches your phone."

"Yeah, all the time. She wants to make sure I'm not recording her. She checks my texts, my messages, everything."

"Jesus, Scott."

"It's fine," he said. "Honestly. It's not that bad."

I promise, Mum, it's all right. The crashing and the mayhem next door, and Mum pretending not to cry.

Lauren grabbed a piece of paper and scribbled Markus's name and a description of his profile photo on Facebook. She slid it across the table, and Scott quickly pocketed it.

"Sir."

Scott looked up to find Beth Vaughn standing at the door. Her face was coated in make-up, so much that the corners of her eyes flaked and white dust danced in the sunlight as she approached. Her lips were curled into a smile, a Casey-like smile. She looked the same whenever she made a joke that had the whole class laughing, mostly at another kid's expense.

"Beth." Scott made himself smile in a friendly way. "Everything all right?"

She paused at the desk. "Not really, sir. I'm sorry, sir."

"Sorry?"

Her smile twitched. "I think you should ask Miss Quintrell to leave. You won't want her hearing this."

Lauren raised an eyebrow. Scott nodded. With a shrug, Lauren rose and left. Beth quickly slipped into the chair.

"The thing is, sir, I just wanted you to know I can reveal the truth any time I want. I can tell the whole world what you did to me."

"What I did to you?"

Monster freak abuser animal beast you deserve it. You deserve it all.

She was beaming. Narrowing her eyes, she looked at him as though he'd asked an obvious question. "You raped me."

26

SCOTT

"This is a serious allegation, Beth."

"I know that, sir. But I can't keep lying. I can't keep this a secret anymore."

Scott had never clenched his teeth so hard. Natalie would often make fun of him for how he'd grit them, telling him he was going to shatter them one day. She'd once even started a 'gritted teeth jar', where Scott had to put in a quid each time he did it. It was an old habit, a way to turn the anger inwards.

But you can't be an angry little kid forever, Natalie had said, laughing.

"If you want to go ahead with this," Scott said, in the steadiest voice he could. He couldn't go on like this. "People will take it seriously. We'll go to court. You'll have to go to the witness stand and describe what I apparently did. Are you ready for that?"

Beth's smile faltered. "I'm not saying I'm going to report you, sir. I just wanted you to know. I *could* report you."

"What a lovely distinction." Scott clapped his hands together, sitting up. "Right then. I think it's time we called the police."

"The police?"

Scott did his best furious teacher face. Which wasn't very difficult, with how badly he wanted to hurt something, someone. Anyone. Flipping the desk would feel so good. Just a release. His thoughts were fragmented. This was Casey; she was finding new ways to torture him.

"Yes, the police," he said. "We'll let them handle this. Make sure you have all the details ready."

"Don't worry." Beth swallowed, eyes flitting here and there. She looked so young for a moment, far younger than fifteen; Scott felt like he was bullying a toddler. "I've got my story all figured out, sir."

"Your story."

"Not my story. What happened. What you did to me."

"Ah, right." Scott picked up his mobile. "And what was that, if you don't mind me asking?"

Beth reached for her sleeve, tugging it down. She'd done it in class many times. Once, Scott was sure he'd seen scars on her wrist; she always wore her long-sleeved sweatshirt, even when it was warm. During PE, Scott had seen her wearing wristbands. Whatever this poor girl was going through, Casey had no right to use her, to twist her.

Right then, Scott wanted to kill her. His own wife. Look what she'd done to him. And now an innocent child.

"You..." Beth paused. "It was after school and you saw me near the shops. You said you wanted to talk to me, and then you grabbed me, sir, and dragged me into an alleyway. It was quick and horrible and then it was over."

"When was this?"

"The fifth of March, sir."

"Where?"

"*Xpress Store*, you know the one, just around the corner from school."

"You sound like you've been coached."

She shook her head. "You raped me, sir. Please stop pretending."

"Wait a second."

He was holding the phone too tightly. He wanted to crush it. Navigating to Casey's name, he clicked *call*. It rang twice and then she answered, sounding chirpy. "Hey, hubby."

"I take it this is you."

"You'll have to be more specific, darling."

"I've got Beth Vaughn in my class."

"I'm afraid I don't know who that is."

"Right."

"But let's say I did..."

Scott's hand went for his stress ball, but he stopped himself. He couldn't let Beth see the effect Casey was having on him.

"Yeah, let's say that," Scott said.

"It's *possible* I got a little peeved, my sweet beautiful husband, when I learned about your little slut playing detective."

Scott closed his eyes for a moment. "Lauren."

"I still talk with the book club girls from time to time. I know what they say about me, how they gossip and bitch, but the truth is they like me. The truth is everybody likes me. I'm a very, very likeable person.

"So you see," she went on. "I can't have some little bitch poking around where she's not wanted. I'd say the book club is off-limits now, wouldn't you?"

Scott turned slightly, lowering his voice. "It's not fair to involve her."

"I'm not the one who raped her."

"Casey–"

"You need to know there's so much more I can do to you.

117

There's so, so much we haven't tried yet. How about this? We'll make a deal."

Scott and Beth stared at each other. She was looking less certain the further the conversation went. The girl had her hands on her knees, fingernails digging into her school trousers.

"Darling, are you there?" Casey said.

"I'm here."

"Did you hear what I said?"

"Yes."

"Well..." She lowered her voice. "Aren't you a teensy bit curious?" She was getting excitable, bubbly in the way that had attracted him to begin with. "I'll delete everything I have. I'll leave you alone forever. But first you have to do something for me."

"What?"

"Rape Beth. And leave the phone on so I can hear. If you do that, I swear I'll leave you alone."

"Goodbye, Casey."

She laughed softly. "Still pretending to be the hero. Fair enough. See you later, honey."

Scott ended the call and glared at Beth. "How much did she pay you?"

"A lot, sir."

"Beth, I want you to know something. Whatever's happening at home, we have ways to help you. You can talk to us. It doesn't have to be me, but we're here."

"Everything's fine at home, sir," Beth said. "The only bad thing that ever happened to me was you raping me."

"Stop saying that," Scott snapped.

"I guess we're done here, sir. Unless you're really going to call the police?"

"Get out of my classroom."

Beth stood and hurried from the room.

The second she was gone, Scott leapt up and threw something at the wall. He wasn't even sure what it was until the pencil pot made a clattering noise, pencils flying everywhere. He spun around, looking for something to break.

Naked photos, naked videos, fine, that was all consensual, embarrassing but consensual, but to go *there*?

He stopped when Lauren approached him, hands raised. "Relax."

"She's gone too far, too bloody far."

"What–"

"You can't go to the book club again. You can't talk to any of them."

"What happened–"

"Lauren!" he shouted, so loudly the kids outside the window must've heard. But he didn't care. He walked up to the teaching assistant, staring down at her. "I mean it. You can't. Never again. Do you understand me? I mean it."

"I'm just trying to help."

"I don't need your help."

She looked at him, seeming wounded. "It sort of looks like you do."

"Stay out of it. I mean it. They've been reporting back to Casey."

"Shit."

"Exactly."

"So what are you going to do?"

"I don't know. I guess I can try to speak with the husband. Just because the book club are reporting back, it doesn't mean *he* will. But there's..."

A lot of ways I can hurt you if I find out, Scottie. Don't you fucking dare.

"I'll just need to be careful," Scott said.

"Let me go then."

"No." Scott turned away so he didn't have to look at the hurt on her face. "You've caused enough damage already."

27

NATALIE

S cott's father had been a high-ranking executive at an advertising agency. Scott would often brag about this, as though his dad's achievements were his own. "You should've heard some of the bonuses he got, Nat."

I hated when he spoke like this, as though money was all that mattered, especially because I knew what would follow... He'd start complaining about our lot, about how neither of us was particularly successful, and somehow it would all become my fault.

I think Scott's upbringing had a lot to do with his ability to switch on the charm when he needed it. His father would host dinners twice or sometimes three times a week, inviting potential clients over to their large home, where Scott's mother would put on a magnificent spread and they'd eat and drink until the early hours.

Scott was often summoned from bed as a mascot of sorts. Apparently he was good at impressions back then; he'd make the whole room erupt with laughter whenever he did an impression of one of the clients, or his dad, or anybody else they asked him to.

I often wish I could go back in time and warn them all. Don't do this. Don't teach him how to pretend. He's going to become far too good at it.

He was good at making people like him. He'd analyse what kind of person they wanted him to be, then he'd simply become that person. With my dad he was respectful and sombre. At school he was professional and approachable.

Once, at my work Christmas party, Scott got talking to one of my colleagues about football. Scott never watches football. But suddenly he was enthusiastic about the sport, being vague enough so my colleague didn't notice Scott wasn't really saying anything.

As far as I know, he never let the mask slip with anybody else. Anybody apart from me.

I remember we were at dinner one evening and Scott started flirting with the waitress. He told her that I was his sister and started asking her about how she'd styled her hair so well, and the woman had smiled and bantered and I'd sat there, not giving a damn, honestly not caring. Let him cheat on me if he wanted; it wasn't like I was innocent there.

Let him target somebody else, let him hurt somebody else.

A cruel thought, perhaps, wishing my hell on another person. But by then I was sick of him. This dinner was a few weeks before The Event, the turning point in our marriage, where his abuse escalated and became outright sadistic. That evening was the starting point; he was evolving into the monster who would make me wish I was dead.

As we were leaving the restaurant, he gripped my forearm. It was on the borderline at first. It could've been affection. But then his fingers got tighter, digging into my skin, until he was crushing my bone.

"Do you even give a shit?" he snarled in my ear, breath hot.

"Aren't you a little bit jealous? I was flirting with her all damn night."

"I feel like you want me to be jealous."

"Well, *something*. You're such a cold cunt."

The word stabbed into me. He'd never called me that before. "What did you want me to do?"

"You should've told that slut to back off. You should've told her I'm taken. You should've pretended to care, at least."

We were standing in the underground car park, next to our car, Scott pushing me up against it.

"Maybe I don't love you anymore. Have you considered that?"

He laughed in that angry manner, as though he could chuckle away the darkness within him. "Get in the car. We'll talk about this at home."

We didn't. Instead, Scott sunk half a bottle of whisky and trashed the living room, ordering me to clean it up.

And I did. Because I was scared. Because I knew that, next time, he'd do more than hurt my arm and call me names.

Casey knew a girl with serious problems when she saw one. She'd spotted Beth leaving Scott's class during one of her spying missions. She liked thinking of them like that, her forays into Scott's school, looking across the yard into the classroom as he paced up and down and pretended to care about the futures of these little brats.

Beth Vaughn had all the signs of a girl who was being abused at home. Casey recognised them straight away.

It hadn't been anything specific about Beth. It was more an *aura*.

Casey smiled as she leaned back in her new recliner chair, the TV playing a film she was barely paying attention to. She was drunk and it was – she glanced at the new, extravagantly expensive clock – only four o'clock.

She didn't care; she swigged some more wine and placed the glass down.

Beth had a shimmering in the air around her. It was everything about her: the way she moved, the way she dressed, the cruel sound of her laughter. Casey had followed the girl home to her shitty flat.

And sure enough, as she'd watched, she'd seen signs of what was happening inside. There he was: the big oh-so strong man, wearing a workman's T-shirt and looking, for all appearances, respectable.

But Casey had eyes like fucking laser beams. She had eyes that went hotter than the *hiss* of an iron: of a phoenix rising. She could pierce his hello-world exterior and see him for the snivelling little kid-touching monster he was. Casey knew all about that, knew how men twisted women, girls, made them their playthings.

That's why Casey had helped her. Approaching her on her way home, she'd walked out right in front of Beth. She was on her own, on a cut-through path that led from the school to a park. Casey felt like hugging her when she stepped back, that cautious guarded look an animal gets. She was clearly smarter than most girls her age.

"Do you want to make some money?"

"Who are you?"

Casey had smirked. "I'm your guardian angel. Do you want the job or not?"

There had been some fun in coaching Beth, warning her not to start bawling like a baby if Scott got a little heated. Casey had warned the girl to make Scott believe it, convince him she'd go public with the story.

But now the fun had waned. That was happening too much lately.

It had only been a couple of weeks, and already she was reminiscing about Scott's face on their anniversary night. She needed excitement. Boredom was death.

She drained her glass and reached for the bottle, but it was already empty. Two hundred pounds, the bottle had cost, the sort people saved for a special occasion. But every day was special. She slid her hand between her legs, thinking of Scott in the dog cage, but it did nothing. With a sigh, she removed her hand, placing it on the arm of the chair.

He'd sent the bitch from his classroom snooping around the book club. Casey had told him the book club girls still talked to her, but that was a lie. They were all so high and mighty, treating Casey like dirt because she'd pursued Scott.

Casey had learned about Lauren's involvement by stalking Fiona's Facebook page. That wannabe hippie freak couldn't resist posting every minor event in her life, as if anybody cared. There were rarely any comments on her posts, except for the ones about her divorce, where she bragged about leaving the only man who would ever love her. A woman like Fiona – boring, anxious, depressing – should've been grateful for whatever she could get.

Fiona had posted about running into her 'new book club friend' Lauren in a café. Apparently they'd had a 'lovely chat' and making new friends made Fiona feel 'so blessed'.

The book club girls couldn't tell Lauren anything worthwhile. Casey felt sure of that. The only person who could do anything was Markus, but he wouldn't dare.

Casey walked across the room, grabbed her phone. She went to Facebook, using her dummy account. She didn't have any accounts under her own name. She hated the way people paraded themselves online, checking in and posting drivel and blah-blah-blahing all over the place.

Sitting, Casey went to Markus's profile. Her ex-husband was a small and tragic-looking man, with a receding hairline and a beanpole figure. His profile photo showed him and Polly: *his* choice, not Casey's. Polly was such a stupid name. The girl was smiling, chubby-cheeked and gap-toothed and seemingly happy.

Casey stared at the girl, trying to make herself feel something. Moving her thumb across the screen, Casey remembered smoothing tears from her daughter's cheeks, back when she'd cared enough to pretend. But there was nothing, just a pit in her belly, seeking *something*.

Giving birth had been an insult. Halfway through, Casey had wanted to reach inside and throttle the thing that was causing her so much pain. She'd screamed at Markus, telling him to make it stop, telling him she didn't want to do this. She should've aborted the fucker. Even the nurses had looked shocked, but Casey's voice wouldn't quieten; she was in agony.

And then it was time to hold her daughter. She thought, maybe, she might feel something when she held her child for the first time.

But she was just a pink bundle of flesh, looking hardly human. Casey quickly passed her to Markus. Markus had stared at her with that annoying hurt look, like he was about to cry.

Now, she rose to her feet. She was drunk, but not drunk enough. And anyway, more alcohol would only make her sloppy and sleepy and she didn't want that. She wanted, more than anything, not to be so bored.

Walking upstairs, she went into her bedroom – *her* bedroom, since Scott rarely slept there anymore – to the new vanity unit. Scott had assembled it for her as she pinged elastic bands at him from the corner. She'd ordered him not to flinch, no matter where they landed. He'd succeeded. That was another problem. Scott was far too docile.

But that was Casey's fault for executing her plan so flawlessly. She'd given him no room to fight back. Sometimes, when they played their games, she was certain the sick little freak enjoyed it.

She opened the drawer and took out the lockbox. Removing the key from her pocket, she opened it, flipped the lid and gazed down at her treasure trove. Her dealer hadn't questioned her influx of cash, allowing her to binge on the most overpriced drug in existence.

She tipped some cocaine onto the back of her hand mirror and cut it into chunky lines. They lay like swollen white slugs. There was at least a gram there, she guessed, but it was difficult to tell. She'd bought ten and had put it all in the same bag.

Snorting the lines, her mind ignited, her body ignited. Suddenly everything was bright and alert and her mouth was numb and she wanted to run, to run fast. She yelled and paced around the room, grinning as she opened and closed her hands, quicker, firmer, barely feeling her freshly manicured fingernails jabbing over and over into her palms.

Here it was: what her brain was lacking. The good chemicals. The ability to feel. More lines, and then she licked her finger and rubbed it all over the hand mirror, pushing the bitter powder between her teeth and over her tongue.

She ran down the stairs, tripped.

Sideways, her shoulder slamming into the wall, and finally her knees crushing into the floor. There was nothing, only faraway pulsing, and suddenly she knew why her father had snorted so much of the stuff. Not *her* stuff. Not the pure. His had been cut with all kinds of shit. His had been pink, yellow, rusty orange. Hers was the cleanest stuff in Bristol, her dealer had assured her.

The front door opened as she was climbing to her feet. Scott stepped in. He looked inflated for the first couple of steps, like he was about to launch into a rant, but he was punctured when he saw her. He deflated. He stared. "Did you fall?"

"My husband, Sherlock Holmes." She walked over to him, staring up into his stupid face. "What games are we going to play today? Do you have anything in mind? Or do you want me to take the lead? Go on. Tell me. What's it going to be?"

"Are you on something?"

"Just some lovely expensive red wine, dear husband. Were

you going to shout at me when you came in? You were wearing a very shouty face."

"I think you should sit down–"

She lashed out, slapping her hand across his cheek. Her palm stung in some distant place and Scott stumbled back, slowly raising his hand to his face. "What the fuck?"

She surged forwards, hitting him again, laughing each time her palm made loud fleshy contact. This was it; this was new. She hadn't hit him yet. She'd made him hurt himself, but she hadn't taken it into her own hands. The thrumming was back, the pulsing, the heat.

"Cowardly fuck," she grunted, shoving him in the chest.

He stumbled and fell against the door. There were *tears* in his eyes.

"What sort of a man are you?" she shouted, imagining what would happen if she'd ever hit her father like this. What would follow. And Scott did nothing, just stared. Weasel. Weak. Men were so *pathetic*. "Come on. Do something. Do something. Fucking *hit me!*"

She threw herself at him, raking her fingernails over his hands when he lifted them. Then he had his hands on her wrists. Oh yes, this was it, this was something. Suddenly the idea of getting bored, ever, seemed ludicrous.

She tossed her hair. "Go on. Take out all that anger. Do whatever you want. I give you permission. Go crazy, Scott."

Darting her hand out, she squeezed onto his crotch, expecting to find him hard. Or at the very least *almost* hard. But he was soft, as feeble as the rest of him.

"I don't want to hurt you," he said.

"Liar."

"I mean it. Please stop hitting me."

"Begging like a little girl." She was rubbing her hand up and down his crotch to no avail. "You can do anything you want.

You can spit on me. You can fuck my ass until I bleed. Anything you want."

"I don't want any of that." His voice was tremoring; he was so close to cracking. "I just want my life back."

She let her hand drop away and stood on her tiptoes, staring into his shimmery eyes. "You are so, so sad."

She punched him in the stomach.

He grunted and fell against the door. Casey spun away, heading for the stairs. She couldn't even look at him. She needed her box, her special box. Maybe some shrooms to make this more interesting. Anything to keep the boredom at bay.

29

SCOTT

Scott took a sick day and drove down to Tess Foster's house. The elderly lady had asked him not to visit during their conversation on the phone, but Scott felt himself getting closer to breaking point. He knew he was risking a lot, deceiving Casey like this – he hadn't told her about the sickie – but he had to know if Casey had been Natalie's lover.

It was the most likely reason Scott could think of for her targeting him. The only truly bad thing he'd done in his life was being so blinded he'd not anticipated his wife's suicide.

Is that really the only *thing?*

Tess had moved from the house near the park to a one-bedroom flat on the other side of Weston-super-Mare, overlooking the seaside. It was a bright day, the promenade full of dog walkers and pedestrians. Scott looked at a happy older couple, walking hand in hand, and felt a pang in his chest. He'd often imagined he and Natalie walking in much the same way. Once they'd laid all their problems to rest.

His face was still sore from when Casey had turned feral. He glanced at himself in the rear-view mirror, hardly recognising his reflection. He looked beaten, like he was ready to quit.

Climbing from the car, he walked across the street and pressed down on her flat's buzzer, muttering a silent thanks to Gary for getting the address.

A minute later, Tess Foster's voice crackled over the intercom. "Uh, hello?"

"Hello, Tess. My name is Scott. We spoke on the phone a few days ago."

"I don't know anybody called Scott."

"We talked about my wife and her..." He cringed. "And her girlfriend."

"She shouted at me."

"That's right."

"And you are?"

"My name's Scott. I was Natalie's husband. Can I come in?"

A pause, and then she said, "No, I don't think I'd like that at all."

"Would you mind coming out here for a second? I promise I won't take up much of your time. I'd like to show you a couple of photos."

"This is really rather irregular."

"I'm sorry."

"Give me a moment."

Scott paced up and down the path, drawing a few odd looks from the passers-by.

The door opened halfway, Tess Foster peering around the edge. From the conversation on the phone, he'd imagined a dishevelled woman, her hair in disarray, her clothing scattered as her thoughts. But she was neat, with combed grey hair and a clean cardigan.

"Yes?" she said. "This is rather irregular."

Scott wondered if she knew she'd repeated herself. He shouldn't be here, bothering this woman.

"You said my wife and her girlfriend shouted at you, back when you lived near–"

"I remember it very well. I'll never forget it. I was so disgusted with how she spoke to me."

"Would you please let me show you some photos? I'm trying to figure out who this other woman was."

"Why?" She opened the door the rest of the way, standing up straighter, suddenly not seeming so meek. Perversely, Scott's first instinct was to flinch away as she stepped forward. "It's a fair question. Shouldn't you be talking to your wife about this?"

"She killed herself. I'm trying to piece together why."

"Oh, how awful. I'm sorry."

Scott didn't mention he'd told her this before. "Will you, please? It won't take long."

She huffed. "Fine. But remember it was dark. And only one of them shouted at me."

Scott took out his phone and swiped to a photo of Natalie. She was standing at the railing of the promenade in Weston, a big smile on her face and the sun at her back. He showed Tess the photo.

"Yes, that's definitely her."

"The one who shouted at you?"

"Gracious, no. That was the other one. I saw her quite often. She'd even visit the park by herself sometimes."

"Okay, thank you." Scott swiped his phone, moving to the photo of Casey. This one was even more painful. He'd taken it a few months after their wedding, at a restaurant, Casey wearing a form-hugging black dress and a loving expression. "What about her? Was this the woman who shouted at you?"

Scott's heart was hurting in his chest. He waited as Tess made *um* and *ah* noises, as though sorting through memories.

"I'm not sure," she finally said. "It was dark. I can't remember. It was cold. She was wearing a hat. I think she was wearing a hat, anyway."

Scott swiped through his phone, finding a photo he'd taken of Casey during winter. It had snowed lightly in Bristol and there was a dusting of it in the park behind her. She'd looked so cute, so adorable, so harmless bundled up in her winter gear.

"Here you go." He showed Tess his phone.

Her eyes glazed and she began shaking her head. "I'm sorry. I can't remember."

"Please. Try."

"I *am* trying. But lately... I'm not sure, S-Sam. I don't know."

Scott swallowed. Her tone was becoming taut. It must be a terrible thing, to have your memory fade away, and worse still to be conscious of the fading.

Scott held the phone in front of her face, unwilling to move it. Something might click in her mind.

"Nothing?" Scott asked.

"It could have been her. I honestly don't know. Oh, God. Tell me something, how can I remember all the lyrics to 'This Little Light of Mine' but not what I had for breakfast?"

Scott didn't move the phone. She was still studying it, as though she'd taken it as a challenge.

She shook her head. "It could be. It mightn't be. I honestly can't say."

"Maybe if I–"

"Nan?"

Scott turned as a man jogged up the lane. He was a head taller than Scott, wide, with the paint-flecked clothes and the solid-looking body of a manual labourer.

"What's this? You're not giving out your bank details again?"

"Oh, stop fussing. It's nothing like that. S-S... this young man wanted my help. You know I never forget a face."

The man eyed Scott. "You need to be careful answering the door to strangers."

She waved a hand. "Always fussing."

"Are you ready?" the man asked.

Tess tilted her head. "Ready?"

"Bingo, remember. I didn't come all this way for nothing."

"Oh, bingo! That's right. Give me a minute, dear."

"All right."

Before Scott could protest, Tess shut the door in his face. The grandson stared down at Scott. He was in his early twenties, Scott guessed, with a skin-fade haircut and a shadow of hair around his jaws.

"What's this, mate? You running a scam?"

"No. I think your grandmother might have some information about my wife. My dead wife. She was having an affair and your grandmother saw them."

He felt conscious of oversharing, but what option did he have other than the truth?

"Hmm. All right. Let's say I believe that." He moved closer. "The thing is, Nan gets a bit upset when you ask her to remember stuff. Her brain's knackered. And she doesn't exactly like being reminded of that, got it?"

"I wasn't trying to upset her–"

"So how about we keep this simple?" Even closer, and Scott could smell sweat and cigarette smoke. "You get out of my face right this second, and I forget you were bothering my nan. That woman basically raised me. I won't see her taken advantage of."

"I wasn't–"

"If you're not up to walking, I reckon we can find another way to make you fuck off. What's it going to be?"

Scott walked across the street and climbed into his car, remembering what Tess had said. It could be and it couldn't be. Which meant he had no more information than when he'd arrived. He had nothing.

30

SCOTT

As Scott drove away, he wondered if he'd have the guts to do it.

He never usually thought of suicide like that. Guts. It wasn't *guts*. It was depression and isolation and terror. But now he wondered. How had Natalie done it, gone through each step, arranging the car and the garage just so? Had she paused at any point, asking herself if she was making the right decision?

Or had she rushed through it all, keen to get it over with?

He remembered an interview with a man who'd survived jumping off a bridge. The man's first reflexive reaction had been regret. He didn't want to die, he realised in those final moments, and then it was too late. The water crashed into him. Lights out. Until he'd miraculously survived, living to carry his message into the world.

Scott had agonised over that interview, desperate to know if Natalie had felt the same instant regret. Or maybe she was smiling, ready to meet her lover at the hangman's broken tree.

It didn't matter. Guts or guilt or terror, Scott could never do it. He couldn't realistically think about it.

He didn't want to die; he just wanted this to end.

The day passed far too quickly; he spent it in a café, off the High Street, paranoid Casey would somehow spot him and realise he wasn't at school. Soon it was time to drive back to Bristol. He gave himself plenty of time. It wasn't like he could tell Casey if there was trouble on the motorway.

He parked down the street with half an hour to spare.

Picking up his phone, he navigated to Facebook, to Markus's profile. Casey's ex-husband who Scott hadn't even bothered to find out about until now. But if a charming, clever, funny, kind, beautiful woman tells him something, why should he instantly doubt it?

But Tess was a dead end; maybe this wouldn't be.

When Scott clicked on the message icon, he saw the green indicator that showed Markus was online.

Scott typed quickly. He hoped Markus wouldn't find it off-putting that his profile photograph didn't show his face; because of his job, Scott had to be careful about social media. It was a photo of the horizon, taken on his and Casey's wedding day. He needed to change that.

Hello Markus. This is going to seem strange. I'm Casey's husband. I thought she loved me, but lately she's been getting abusive. I'm talking full-on physical assaults now, mate. Can we talk?

He clicked send without giving himself time to read the message over. He didn't like describing what was happening as abuse. When she'd been hitting him, he hadn't felt like a man at all. But this was about practicality; he couldn't be vague. There was no way Markus could ignore something so clear, surely.

Three dots appeared, vanished, appeared... vanished. Until finally the message came through.

Can I call you?

Scott typed quickly.

Yes.

A moment later, the Messenger screen changed to a call. Scott quickly answered it and put it on loudspeaker, glancing around the street. Kids were coming home from school. A man rode his bike. There was no sight of Casey.

"Hello, Scott."

"Hello."

Markus sighed. "Is that true?"

"It's true. I'm sorry to spring this on you."

Markus sighed again. "Casey..."

"You don't sound surprised."

"No," Markus said. "I'm not sure what I can do to help."

Scott rested his head against the steering wheel, feeling like all the energy was seeping out of him.

"Anything," Scott said. "Anything you can do."

"Is it that bad?"

"Worse."

"I really am sorry."

"Can we meet?" Scott thought he might be able to get more out of him in person.

"For what? I called because I wanted to tell you I'm sorry. But I meant what I said. There's nothing I can do to help. She's left us alone for more than a year now. That's the best I can hope for."

He sounded just like Scott.

"You're scared," Scott said.

"You said you were Casey's new husband. You said she was getting abusive."

"Yeah."

"So there's your answer. I'm not sure how far she's taken things with you, but... She's capable of a lot, that woman."

"Please meet with me. Nobody else knows what this is like." Scott wouldn't reveal his true reason for wanting to meet: to find out how Markus had made Casey back off. "Hello?"

"I'm still here."

Scott waited, giving the street another quick scan. If Casey found him while he was on the phone, she'd force Scott to show her before he deleted the conversation history. Then the *games* would start.

"The thing is, she can't know," Markus said. "I can't have her in my life again."

"She'll never know. I swear."

"I still don't get why you want to meet."

"To talk."

"We're talking now."

Scott ran a hand through his hair. His body was coated in sweat. It always was lately. "Please."

Markus paused for a long time. When he spoke, his voice trembled. "I just wish she'd stop. Why does she have to be like this? Why does she have to make everybody's life hell?"

"I don't know. The truth is, I don't know a bloody thing about her."

"Polly, my daughter, she has netball on Thursday. You can come by then if you want, but like I said, I've got no idea what good it'll do."

His daughter, not Casey's. And could Scott blame him if he thought that way?

"You understand. You're the only person. That's all I need. I can't talk to anybody else about this."

That was a half-truth. He could talk to Gary and even to Lauren, but neither of them knew what it was like, to fear his own wife. And, once they were face to face, it would be easier to get more information out of him. Scott would beg if he had to.

"I'll message you my address," Markus said. "Thursday at half past three work for you?"

"Yes, that should be fine." Scott wouldn't think about how he'd get to that meeting without alerting Casey's suspicions. One problem at a time. "But don't text me. Just tell me now. I'll get a pen and paper."

"She checked my phone too." He paused, then cleared his throat. "You ready?"

Scott wrote down the address and put it in the glove compartment. After saying goodbye, he drove the rest of the way and parked up.

Opening the front door, he smelled vanilla-scented candles. The lights had been turned down and soft jazz played.

Casey appeared at the living-room door, wearing a silk dress that shifted as she approached him. Her hair was immaculate. She smelled like heaven.

Scott took a step back.

"That's fair." Casey bowed her head. "I was drunk yesterday. It's no excuse, but... I'm sorry. I never should've hit you. I hate myself for it."

Scott *knew* she was lying, and yet he had to remind himself. Her performance was so convincing. He fought the urge to embrace her.

She flipped a switch. She could do it again. There was nothing here, nothing real, not like with Natalie.

"I made us dinner," Casey said. "I know it's not enough to make up for what I did. But it's a start, isn't it?"

Scott couldn't exactly tell her no. "It's a start."

"Well, come on then!" she exclaimed, making him believe, for a corrupted moment, she truly did want to make amends.

31

CASEY

C asey regretted the way she'd behaved the previous day. It wasn't how she wanted things to go.

Only weak people relied on drugs to be able to enjoy themselves. Use them to enhance the experience, fine, but to allow herself to sink into a hole of boredom, a hole she could only climb out of with cocaine?

No. Fuck that.

She was going to have some fun whilst sober. And she was *completely* sober. Not even a glass of red or a little blunt. The comedown had hit her savagely. Apart from one errand, which was necessary, she'd spent the entire day in bed with a cold flannel on her forehead, waiting for the feeling to pass.

Memories had attacked her, fuelled by the cocaine-induced depression. She saw her father and his hands, his dirty nicotine-stained fingers. She saw teddy bears piled up against the door, and heard them collapse, so much louder in her mind than they'd been in reality.

What's this you've done, princess?

She was nobody's princess.

Walking into the kitchen, she smiled at him. She'd prepared

a bottle of champagne in a shiny silver bucket. The casserole was on the counter, covered by a tea towel, and she'd turned the lighting down low like the rest of the house.

"Why don't you put on some other music while I dish up?"

"Uh, sure."

Scott looked around for the Bluetooth speaker. Casey had purposefully placed it in the corner of the room, as far away from the casserole dish as possible, so Scott wouldn't see what she was doing.

When he walked across the room, she moved to the counter and grabbed his special plate from the microwave, removing the tinfoil. She gave it a sniff. It smelled edible. If there was a stink, she was sure the vanilla candles and the smell of her food would cover it.

Guitar strings plucked in the air. A man's deep voice joined it a moment later. Casey turned to find Scott staring at her, childish defiance on his face. It took her a second to realise what he was doing.

He was playing their song. Which really wasn't their song. It was a song Casey had pretended to like, forcing tears as she listened to it, as the singer droned on about soulmates and destiny and a bunch of other made-up rubbish.

"Did it ever mean anything to you?" Scott asked.

Casey carried the plates over, careful not to mix them up. "Of course it did. We fell in love to this song. It makes me want to cry just thinking about it."

She swayed softly, as the drums beat in the background, the man's voice rising. He was prattling about how he knew this girl was the one for him, just a look, a glance, and their fate was sealed. The song fitted them perfectly. Scott had known he loved her after a couple of weeks.

As she rocked, she began to weep. Summoning the tears was easy. She did what she always did; she became a little girl again.

She remembered what it felt like to be afraid. She had to go back to when she was very young, maybe around eight or nine, before she'd realised how useless tears were.

You cannot tame the savage in me. You cannot tame the lioness waiting to break free. I was born with an edge. I was birthed sharp.

Her chest started to hurt and she kept swaying, almost feeling something, *almost*. That was the thing. Casey wasn't crying right now. It was a child someplace faraway. Nobody would ever understand that. It wasn't her fault.

She'd hoped Scott might take the bait, come to her, hold her. It would make it all the sweeter when she revealed the truth.

Scott stared. "Am I allowed to start eating yet?"

"Yes." She grabbed some kitchen towel and dabbed her eyes, and then sat down. "Let's eat."

"Was that real?" Scott picked up his cutlery.

"What an odd question."

"Right."

"Love you." She smiled. "Aren't you going to say it back?"

He looked at her miserably. "I love you too."

"How sweet. Go on then. Before it gets cold."

He waited until she started to eat. He thought she was going to poison him; or he wanted to make it seem that way, a juvenile protest. She shrugged and tucked in, forking a potato slice and a piece of chicken, chewing enthusiastically. That was one good thing she got from her childhood. She became a decent cook, even if she didn't particularly enjoy it. Her dad had been terrible in the kitchen.

Casey had forgotten something. "Scott, can I use your phone for a second? Mine's dead."

He grinned. She read the message. It was like, *Ah, so we're not pretending with everything*. She took his phone, opened it, and made sure he wasn't recording her. She'd often randomly search him. But she decided to leave it. He knew better than that, surely.

Casey carried on eating, trying not to watch Scott too eagerly. Finally he pierced a bit of meat and put it in his mouth. She'd made the sauce thick, cloying, so it would stick to everything, making it difficult to tell what was what.

Scott chewed and swallowed, then went on eating. Casey supposed that made sense. A lot of taste happened in the mind. It didn't matter. She'd let him eat as much as he could handle.

"So how was your day?" she asked.

His fork paused in its path to his mouth, just for a moment. "Fine. Same old, same old."

"I hope none of the students gave you any problems."

He shook his head. "No, all good."

"Well, that's great. I'm happy for you."

They ate quietly for a time, as the song changed and changed again. Scott had almost finished his dish. He probably wanted to get this over with.

"I went by the school today, actually," Casey said.

Scott's fork clattered in the bowl. Sauce spattered his shirt. "Oh."

"It was so strange. I had a cheeky look in your classroom. It's so well-situated for surprise visits, isn't it? A street-facing beauty, so easy to check in."

"Yeah." He opened and closed his hand, the burned bandaged one, not the ugly-as-fuck one with the missing pinkie finger. "I guess it is."

"You weren't there."

Casey regretted not smoking a little, at least. She should've been laughing, or at least holding back laughter. Or she should've *wanted* to laugh. But there was nothing, the barest flickering ember. All day she'd looked forward to this. And now it seemed like a big anti-climax.

145

She'd come too far. She had to press on.

"Where *were* you, Scott?"

"I needed some time. I drove to Weston and I sat in a café and read a bloody book, all right? I just needed a change of scenery... What's happening here, with us, it takes a lot out of me."

"Hmm. Is that the whole truth?"

"Yes."

She studied his face. He was lying. Perhaps she could make him tell her, but she wasn't sure. She didn't want him to become *too* used to the punishment. He might become like Casey had been once, docile, staring dead-eyed up at the ceiling, a million miles away. She couldn't allow him to detach.

"I don't believe you."

"I swear," he said. "On Natalie's life... on Natalie. That was all I did."

"Because you loved Natalie so, so much."

He flinched. "I did. You know that."

"Right." She rolled her eyes, suppressing the niggle, the note of imperfection in this grand song. "Do you want to know what I did when I realised you'd lied to me?"

His lips were trembling.

"I'm not much of a religious person," she went on. "But today, it was like a gift from God. As I was leaving the school, there it was, lying on the ground, waiting for me."

"A gift from God," he whispered, and Casey swore for a second he was about to go all Jesus-freak on her. "What was it?"

"A dead rat."

He shook his head. "Don't be stupid."

"I thought you might say that."

Casey stood and walked to the sink, reaching into the underside counter and taking out the bundle of tissue paper. She carried it to the table, unwrapping it until the rat's bony carcass fell away. It was nothing but a spine and ribs, all the meat stripped clean, all the hair gone, with no tail.

"Everything that isn't on that." Casey pointed at the carcass. "Is in that." She pointed to Scott's plate, and his sickened face made her giggle. It was a wonderful thing. She wanted to hug him for making her laugh. "Or that, I should say." She gestured at his belly.

"This is a joke."

"Is it?"

Scott's hand flew up to cover his mouth. He ran for the hallway, for the downstairs bathroom.

It was too tempting. Casey stuck her foot out.

He fell flat on his face, the vomit erupting from between his clasped fingers. Casey's laughter grew; this was it. She could feel it. *Yes.* It was happening. He rolled onto his side and puked all over the floor, shuddering, as blood streamed sideways down his face from his nose.

"Why?" the wretch moaned, voice tangled with vomit and crying and his weeping nostrils. "Just tell me why. Was it you? Were you and Natalie together? Is that it?"

"Together?" Casey smirked. "Is that what you think?"

"Please. Just tell me. I deserve to know."

"Oh, sweet baby." She knelt, softly stroking her fingers through his hair. "Look at you. But it can get so much worse." He *had* to know that. He should've fought her; it was beneath contempt, his lack of action. "No money. No career. No hope. No self-respect. No friends. No home. Nothing. And then, if you ask very nicely, I might put you out of your misery."

She stood quickly, stepping away from him. "Clean this mess up. You're disgusting."

He stared, lips shiny with vomit, nose shiny with blood, eyes shiny with tears.

"Don't look at me like that. You're the idiot who married a stranger."

She was tempted to kick him in the gut, but she was barefoot and didn't want to hurt her toes.

Returning to the table, she continued eating. Scott quietly climbed to his feet and walked across the room, grabbing some kitchen towel and cleaning his face.

"Honey? I need another five thousand. I hope that's okay."

"It's fine."

"And no more surprise sickies, deal?"

He placed the dirty kitchen towel on the counter and grabbed some more, holding it against his nose. "No more. I promise."

32

SCOTT

Scott felt like he was sleepwalking during the next couple of days at work.

He was certain he could still taste the rat, even after brushing his teeth several times. He bought some mouthwash and kept it in the top drawer of his desk, swilling it every chance he got. Maybe she'd been bluffing, he told himself, but he knew that was a lie. Casey didn't bluff. She just did. And the stinking rat carcass had proved it.

Casey waited outside for him both days, leaning against the car, looking glamorous with her designer sunglasses perched atop her head. As he approached her, he tried to match this version with the woman who hit him, but he couldn't.

She was like an expert impressionist; she was a bloody mascot, not a person at all.

To make things even more difficult, Beth Vaughn was acting up in class. She'd taken out her mobile phone several times, shooting him a challenging look. Scott pretended not to see, as he imagined Beth running to the headteacher's office – probably with some fake tears, perhaps even with some fake blood – and telling her story.

On the third day, Scott asked Lauren to wait behind. It was the meeting with the husband the next day.

Lauren walked over to the desk, pity radiating from her like a stench. Scott shrunk away from it. They hadn't spoken much since he'd snapped at her, reverting to their professional relationship, but Scott had caught her looking at him from time to time.

"I'm sorry," Scott said. "I shouldn't have snapped at you. None of this is your fault."

She nodded. "Don't worry about it."

"Really. I mean it."

Her laughter sounded nervous. "Take it easy, honestly. It's fine. You don't look good, Scott."

He didn't have to ask her why. Scott had busted his nose by falling into the fridge; it had been late and he'd slipped on the tiles, crushing his face against the handle. That was the story he told in the staffroom, to the kids, even somehow making a joke out of it. He was weirdly proud of how he could wall that part away, focus on the kids.

He'd always been good at separating home and work life.

Each morning his reflection gazed back at him like a ghoul, both eyes faintly black. His cheeks were gaunt, hollow.

"I need a favour," he said.

Lauren sat down, watching him.

"I've arranged to meet with the husband, Markus, tomorrow. But I can't go. You've probably seen Casey waiting for me after school."

"I have. Standing there like one of those *Real Housewives*. Have you ever watched that? My partner loves it, but it drives me crazy. So much arguing about nothing."

Scott let the comment pass. "Will you meet with him for me? I can pay you."

"I don't want your money. Of course I'll go."

"Of course," he repeated. "I still have no idea why you're being so helpful."

"Are you complaining?"

"No. I just... why?"

"I've told you. I'm a curious person. I like you. Not everything has to be complicated."

Scott ran a hand through his hair, winced when his fingers brushed against the sore spot. Meat tenderisers worked just as well on people as dead things.

"He's expecting me," Scott went on. "I'd message him to let him know plans have changed, but..."

Lauren nodded, and Scott was relieved he didn't have to explain. Casey was checking his phone constantly. She'd started searching him more regularly, not that Scott would ever try to record her now. It wasn't even the video and the photos anymore; it was her, this devil he was married to, and all the painful things she'd do to him.

He thought of the church near their house; he'd been eyeing that one every day, staring out the window, feeling a strange pull. Like he could give his problems to somebody else, something else: bigger, stronger, more capable of carrying them.

"You have to be careful," he went on. "You can't be followed. And Markus needs to know he can't tell Casey, under any circumstances. That's important."

"I'm worried about you." Lauren leaned forwards, looking solidly at him. "Maybe this is all too much. Maybe you should just let her release the videos. I know it'll change your whole life. I get that. But Scott... look at you. You flinch every time a door closes. You're letting the kids walk all over you."

He rolled his stress ball from one side of the table to the other. He couldn't squeeze it; both hands hurt from Casey's games. "I haven't come this far just to give up."

"Come this far?" Lauren narrowed her eyes. "What have we

accomplished, really? From where I'm sitting it seems like the only thing that's changed is you. She's breaking you–"

"You're telling me shit I already know," he snapped.

Lauren shrugged. "All right. Have you got Markus's address? What time are you supposed to visit him?"

Scott reached into his top drawer, past the mouthwash, and brought out the piece of paper. He slid it across the desk. Lauren tucked it into her pocket.

"He has to help," Scott said. "She's left him alone for over a year, he said. He must have a way to make her stop."

"I hope so, Scott."

33

NATALIE

The first time Scott hit me, the emotion I felt most of all was surprise. I barely felt the pain: the contact of his fist against my cheekbone. I *heard* it, the flesh-on-flesh collision, but the sensation seemed distant. As I fell to the floor of our living room – narrowly missing the edge of the coffee table – I remember thinking, *He didn't just hit me. He wouldn't go that far.*

Apart from sometimes gripping onto my arm, he'd never been physically violent before. We'd been arguing about his work party.

Apparently I was flirting with one of his colleagues, which was laughable. The colleague was a man, twenty years older than me. He was the English teacher and we'd been talking about books, that's all, but Scott saw me from across the room and gave me this dark look. I knew something bad would happen when we got home, but I hadn't expected this.

He came at me from behind, bringing his hand around in a wide arc, so I only saw the punch at the last second.

Once I was down, he loomed over me, spittle coating his

lips, his eyes glassy from all the drinks he'd greedily gulped that night. "Teach you to be a slut, won't it?"

"I didn't do anything." My mouth throbbed as I spoke, my words coming out jumbled. "We were talking about *Tess of the d'Urbervilles*. I think you've really hurt me."

I stood slowly, but apparently I was supposed to remain on the floor. Scott leapt at me and–

Well, he did very bad things. He went at me for far too long. He used his feet and his fists and, when I was a mangled mess on the floor, he used his final weapon. He used it roughly and it hurt and I bled and there was so much agony, and then I was someplace else; I was at the hangman's broken tree, and her hand was in mine, her soft and welcoming hand.

My love, my only true love, she was smiling radiantly into my eyes. Her hands slipped around my hips and she pulled me into a kiss. As my husband committed his sins – as Father would put it – I disappeared into the fantasy.

I thought about lying in the summer grass, braiding her hair as she sent soft song notes fluttering through the air. I imagined the feel of her body against mine, the security of her arms around me, the feeling of melting together: the certainty nothing could ever hurt us.

"Moan, Nat. Moan. *Now*."

His voice punctured the fog, and my mouth did what he wanted. But then I retreated again. We were walking beneath the shadow of the hangman's broken tree, the sturdy trunk leaning against the railing. I thought about her face as we carved our names into the stone wall, the glee making her lips twitch.

On and on, he kept going, and there were noises, wet and sickening. I pushed them all away.

I was with her, the only woman I'd ever need. She was trailing her fingers down my arm and her breath was warm against my neck.

It wasn't Scott. It was her, her, my beautiful perfect *her*.

"We should get married," she'd said once, as we both lay sweaty and sorely contented in a hotel room.

"We can't."

"Why?"

"My parents..."

She'd tenderly kissed my forehead. "You can't let them rule you forever."

"You don't understand. They'd never talk to me again."

"It must be a strange god," my earthbound angel whispered in my ear, as her fingers trailed up my naked thigh, "to care about what body parts people use to express their love."

"We're an abomination." I moaned as her fingertips pushed against the still-tender place. "We're bound for Hell, both of us..."

34

LAUREN

Markus must've been waiting for the doorbell to ring. The moment Lauren pressed down on it, the door swung open. He was a small thin man, with brown-grey fuzz smoothed across his balding pate. Lauren guessed he was in his mid-thirties – his face was young – but his haircut, combined with his beige sweater, made him seem older.

He looked her up and down. "You're not Scott."

"He asked me to come."

"Why?"

"How much do you know?"

"About him and Casey?" Lauren nodded, and Markus blew out a long breath. "I know she's... she's doing what she does, what she did to me, but to him."

"So there you go. That's why he can't come."

"I see."

"Can I come in?"

He looked around his garden, back down the narrow hallway, and then finally at Lauren again. "Who are you? To Scott, I mean?"

There was no way she could answer this honestly. Even if

she explained her connection, Markus would still question her motives. He'd wonder why she was getting involved. And it wasn't like Lauren was going to tell him about the idea she was toying with: using whatever leverage she gained to make Scott tell her the truth.

"I work with him. I'm his friend. That's why he asked me to do this; I can report back anything I learn. School is the only place she leaves him alone."

Markus stood aside, waving his hand. The hallway was neat, photos of a little girl hanging from the walls, some of them with Markus and some of them with an elderly couple. "Your parents?" she asked.

Markus nodded. "Polly loves them. Would you like a cup of tea?"

"Sure, two sugars, please."

They sat in the living room, Markus in the armchair and Lauren on the sofa. There was a big display unit opposite them, glass, with more photos inside. Lauren didn't spot any of Casey. But of course, there wouldn't be.

"How bad is it for him?" Markus asked, after taking a sip of his tea.

"Pretty bad. He doesn't tell me everything. But he doesn't have to."

"Can't he leave?"

Lauren shook her head, quickly explaining about the blackmail material.

"That's dreadful. Evil."

"We need to make her stop. Fiona, I'm not sure if you know her?"

"From the book club."

"She said you had an argument once. Casey was screaming in your face and then you whispered in her ear, and suddenly she backed off. What did you say?"

"She was so, so good in the beginning," Markus said. "We were so happy. For months. And then one day she just hit me on the back of the head. Without warning. Imagine that. Imagine you love this woman. You think you're going to spend the rest of your life with her. And then, just like that, she turns violent. I thought I'd imagined it at first."

Lauren took a sip of her tea, watching, saying nothing. He clearly wanted to talk, and she wasn't in a rush.

"After that, it only got worse. I couldn't even... even *acknowledge* it for a long time. Do you know what that's like, hiding something, even from yourself?"

Lauren did know, but she hadn't felt like it since she was perhaps fourteen or fifteen years old. She liked to think she'd grown; she was twenty-four now. She felt like she was finally becoming herself. More assertive, but not in an ugly way. She was doing this, wasn't she? Even when she'd been told no.

"Yes," Lauren said after a pause.

"I was so ashamed," he went on. "No matter what anybody says, it's embarrassing, being beaten up by a woman. I bet you think that sounds sexist."

Lauren smiled softly. "Why do you say that?"

"I don't know. You seem very modern, I guess."

Lauren guessed he meant her dyed hair and her outfit. She was wearing some chic dungarees, with heavy combat boots. Some idiot – a cruel person who thankfully was no longer her friend and would never be again – had once called her a cliché because of her outfit choices. It always annoyed her, really pissed her off honestly, because she liked dressing like this. She wasn't *making a statement* or anything else. She was simply wearing what she wanted. But some people couldn't get past the surface level. People like that, who never bothered to peer deeper, led the most miserable and narcissistic lives.

But she didn't think Markus was that sort of person.

"I don't think you're sexist. I think you were scared."

"It's just... it'd be so much easier if she was a man. Mentally, I mean. It makes you feel so, so small."

"That makes sense."

"How much do you know about her childhood?"

"Nothing," Lauren said.

"She rarely talked about it, but a few years ago, we got into this huge argument and she started ranting. Her mum died when she was seven, and she loved her mum; that was the only time I saw genuine emotion, I think, in hindsight. The only time she wasn't pretending. When she was talking about her mum. But then the story would change."

"Change?"

He laid his tea down, gripping his knees. "She'd tell me she killed her parents. Or that her mum is still alive; then it was that she'd done something to her dad, and she'd make these... This is going to sound like a joke."

"Go on."

"Hissing noises," he said, flinching as though the memory was striking him. "There's so much about her that feels..."

Lauren took another sip of her tea. Markus didn't speak for a long time, staring at the TV; no, it was the cabinet, at one of the drawers.

"It feels like an act," he said finally. "I kept thinking, well, she's going to snap back to normal now. Or she can't be serious. Or... there must be an explanation, something to make it okay."

He was staring at the drawer again.

"The only part which didn't change was the stuff her dad did to her. I feel dirty even talking about this."

"I get it," Lauren said. "I don't want to pry."

Too much.

She felt like a little girl again, her dad smiling at her as she traipsed through the house in her long detective's jacket, magnifying glass raised. Her parents had always been so loving, so accepting; it had never changed. She was on the case now. Dad might be disappointed if she told him, but she bet he'd be a little proud too.

"I don't think she even knows who she is," Markus said. "How can a person be convincing and ridiculous at the same time?"

Lauren shook her head. "I honestly don't know. But people have bad childhoods all the time. I know plenty myself. They are some of the most loving people I've ever met. What happened to them, it made them kinder; it made them..."

"Go on," Markus murmured.

Lauren suddenly felt conversationally overdressed; she was speaking with the tenor of a sermon. "It's not even that it *makes* them anything. I think a bad childhood can bring out the bad, but I think a person can also shrug it off, and just... just be the good person they were all along. That's all."

"So maybe Casey was born bad, and made worse."

"Yeah. I guess so. But if her story changes, who knows?"

"Who knows," Markus repeated. "But *I* know who she is."

His voice trembled and he glared at the drawer, like he was trying to move it with his mind.

"What is it, Markus?" Lauren asked, gesturing at it.

He looked at her sharply. "I'm just thinking."

"And I'm still wondering what magic words you said to make Casey back off."

"I don't see what good this can do," he said. "I only agreed to meet with Scott so I could tell him... Tell him I'm sorry, I guess. Tell him I'm so fucking sorry."

"Telling him sorry won't help him. He's got two black eyes, Markus."

He flinched. "Really?"

"They're faded a little, but yeah. He's telling a hilarious story about how he tripped and fell, telling it to anybody who will listen. It's almost like he doesn't believe it himself."

I will get what I need out of you. Somehow.

Lauren wondered at this monomaniacal purpose which had taken hold of her. She liked it, and suddenly she thought maybe teaching wasn't for her; she thought about being a police officer. It was a random funny sort of thought, as she'd never considered it before. Could she do it one day?

"I can't help him."

"Why not?"

Markus stared at her blankly. "Why do you think?"

"I'm not asking you to do anything. Just tell me what you said. Fiona said she backed off like *that*." Lauren snapped her fingers. "Why? How?"

"You don't know her," Markus said, rubbing one hand over the other. "Not like I do. I won't even let Polly see her real mum. I never will."

"See her how, Markus?"

Lauren's heart was thumping in a pleasant way. She wanted to help this man. But she needed him to help her far more. Scott was either an innocent man, and so deserved help; or he was guilty as fuck and deserved everything he was getting. But Lauren had to be sure.

"If I tell you *anything*..."

Lauren swallowed. She felt a little sick; the pleasantness was rapidly fading. "You can't live your entire life scared of her. And you shouldn't feel right, Markus, knowing another man's out there, getting beaten up and God knows what else, when you could help."

He was staring at the floor sullenly, and Lauren wondered if it was too far. She said it anyway. "Is that the sort of example you want to set for Polly?"

"You don't know what you're saying," Markus said bitterly. "You have no bloody clue. Not a single one."

"Give me one then," Lauren said.

"You're going to be sorry." He laughed harshly as he strode around the coffee table and leaned down. He opened the drawer and brought out a small lockbox. Looking at her, he nodded. "I need you to turn around."

"Really?"

He nodded.

"All right. Fine."

She stood, facing the window: the voile made the passing dog walker into two silhouettes. When she heard movement behind her, she slowly peered over her shoulder. Markus had his back turned: another drawer, this one in the display cabinet.

He turned; Lauren snapped her head around.

Markus dropped the lockbox on the table. "We were burgled a few years ago. I installed security cameras out front and back. I didn't tell Casey, so either she didn't know or she didn't care."

"What did she do?"

"I need to get my laptop. It's just in the hall."

He stared at her as if to say *don't steal the lockbox*. Walking quickly, he strode through the door. Lauren's hand actually twitched, as if telling her to grab it, whatever it was. It was the whole reason she was here.

But then he was back. He sat and opened the lockbox, bringing out a portable hard drive. "I can't explain it. I can't even think about it. But I can show you.

"I'll mute the sound," he said, waving her over as he stood. "Tell me when it's finished. I can't watch."

Lauren sat, took the laptop, a feeling of danger coming over her.

"Can I unmute the sound?" she asked.

Markus groaned, pacing over to the opposite chair. "You'll change your mind."

Lauren looked at the still frame of the security footage. When she clicked play, she saw a cat come into frame, a gorgeous British Shorthair, and then Casey walked into view. She was stumbling strangely, wearing an ill-fitting dress flecked with dirt; she had a garden tool in her hand, a trowel.

Markus was right; Lauren muted the sound.

But she watched, even as her instincts tried to make her look away. She watched as Casey marched over... And she did evil and terrible things to the poor cat. She was laughing as she did it, her lips parted, as she paraded around the garden. The kitty struggled. Casey didn't care.

It lasted a couple of minutes, but it felt like forever.

At the end of the clip, Casey stared down at the lifeless lump on the ground. Her expression was vacant.

Tears streamed down Lauren's cheeks. She was thinking of her own cat, Zora.

"That bitch." Lauren stood, shaking all over. "That monster. That pathetic, that, that..."

She deflated, sitting back, as the screen went dark. Lauren knew the video would be imprinted on her mind forever. Casey had done it all so casually, so matter-of-factly, as though killing an animal was just another chore. Lauren could imagine Casey going inside and washing her hands, humming a tune, as the innocent creature lay lifeless in the garden.

"Is it over?" Markus asked.

"Yes." Lauren forced the word past her tears. "She doesn't deserve to breathe. She should be *executed*."

"Agreed." Markus swiftly walked over and grabbed

163

everything. "Polly loved that cat. I had to tell her he ran away. When I confronted Casey, she didn't care. She laughed, telling me to grow up, telling me caring about pets wasn't healthy."

"Can I make a copy of this video?"

Markus's demeanour changed. "No."

"Why?"

"She'll know it came from me. I can't risk that. I'm finally getting my life back. Me and Polly, we're in a good place."

"We won't release it. We'll threaten her with it."

Or Lauren would use it on Scott to get the full story about Natalie. If that was even worth it now; everything seemed pale and pointless after the video.

"I'm guessing that's what you did, at the book club?" Lauren pressed.

Markus glared. "Her whole life is based on tricking people. It's hard to do that when they've seen you kill a cat."

She wanted to tear Casey's throat out; she wasn't used to violent thoughts like this. But cats were the most wonderful creatures, with entire personalities, each one unique, skilled and graceful and beautiful and loving if they're in the right mood.

To do what she did...

"Threaten her, fine," Markus stated flatly. "Then what? She'll still know it came from me. I know Casey. She'll want revenge. I can't–"

"Without this video, we have nothing. She'll keep torturing Scott."

"*I can't!*" Markus exploded.

Lauren leapt to her feet, hands raised. "Take it easy."

"I can't," he repeated, quieter. "Get out of my house. I've done my part."

"You haven't given me anything we can use to make her stop. How is that doing your part?"

"Get out of my house."

"You want her to keep hurting Scott. It keeps her distracted. You're happy for her to kill him as long as it keeps her away from you, is that it?"

"I said *get out!*"

Lauren marched for the door. Markus held the hard drive behind his back, as though Lauren was going to steal it.

She walked onto the street, her throat tight. The poor cat. That crazy *bitch*.

Lauren needed to get her hands on that video.

35

CASEY

Casey laid the flowers on her mother's grave. The headstone was clear, making the words easily readable. *Loving mother, devoted wife.*

It was true. Casey's mother had loved her. No matter how many years passed, no matter how misty memories of her became, she knew that. Her father didn't start with his filth until Mum was gone, and before that Casey remembered so much warmth and affection. She remembered the smell of her mother's perfume and hugging close to her body and a broad light-filled smile.

But then there was the other part. Devoted wife.

That was true too, as far as Casey could remember; family photo albums indicated the same. She'd stood by this man, who *must* have shown some signs of who he really was. Somewhere along the way, there must've been a comment, a look, something that revealed his sick desire. Casey may have her fun, but she'd never hurt a child.

She looked back at the car. Even from there, she could see that Scott was trembling. She knew sweat would be flowing down his forehead, his cheeks. She gave him a thumbs up and turned to the other grave.

There lay dear Daddy. His headstone was overgrown with weeds, the liar's letters covered in grime. He'd never loved anything except for the worm between his legs.

"Do you remember the day you told me you were ill? You looked at me like you expected me to care. You had tears in your eyes, you pathetic fuck. Do you remember what I did?"

Her dad had told her while he was doing the ironing. She was twenty-three, and in the years since her girlhood they'd silently agreed to pretend none of it had ever happened. It was like he thought they could bury it: he could still be a good dad despite all that. But that wasn't how life worked.

Something had snapped in her. All that pain, all that humiliation, all the wrong. It had thundered up inside of her and she'd grabbed the iron, smashing him across the mouth. He'd grunted, fallen, and then Casey was on him. She pushed the iron against his neck, cackling as his skin sizzled, screaming words she couldn't remember now; they were lost in the *hiss* of his flesh.

But she remembered the sense of the words, the general meaning. She was telling him she'd never forgive him. He couldn't make it all go away. She was glad he was going to die.

He'd begged her to stop, but she kept on, tearing his trousers down. He tried to fight her; each time, she thumped him in the face with the iron. He was crying like a child, like she'd cried, and Casey knew this was right. She should've done this a long time ago.

Pulling down his boxers, she pressed the iron against the thing. He'd wept and lashed out at her, but she pushed harder, harder, ignoring the strikes against her face. By the end, his dick was scorched and mangled. She couldn't believe she'd ever felt threatened by it.

Standing, she'd stared down at him, his neck covered in deep red welts, his hands moving to cover himself.

"What's the matter? You want some privacy?" She threw the ironing board on top of him and kicked him in the stomach. "Whatever medicine they offer you, whatever treatments, tell them no."

Casey had toyed with violence before that, especially as a girl when she'd done all manner of interesting things with the neighbourhood animals. But this was the first time she truly understood how magnificent physical violence could be.

"Love you, Mum," she said now, rising to her feet.

She spat on her father's grave, and then walked back towards the car.

She'd been right about Scott. His face was coated in sweat.

Climbing into the driver's seat, she reached over and took his wrist. Acupuncture needles protruded from the skin between his fingers and his thumb, dozens of them criss-crossing.

"Is it bad?" She flicked one of them and he gulped. "I'll take that as a yes."

With a sigh, she began to remove them. It was no good. The rat had given her a bit of a thrill, but since then there'd been nothing. In a way, she envied her father. He'd never grown tired of what he did to her. But that was because he was far less clever, needed less stimulation. He was also nowhere near as imaginative as Casey.

She dropped the needles onto the dashboard, starting the car with a smile. "Shall we get some dinner on the way home? I'm starving. And maybe after you can take me shopping. Doesn't that sound like a lovely evening?"

Scott stared straight ahead. "Yes."

36

GARY

"They're *finally* asleep," Gary said, walking into the living room.

Aissa smiled from the sofa, her hands wrapped around a mug of hot chocolate. Gary always felt a pang of love when he saw her like that; it was something *more* than love too, the everyday normality of it lighting him up in some magical way. Or maybe he was just dog-tired after getting the kids to sleep.

He dropped down next to Aissa, wrapping his arm around her and laying his cheek against the top of her head.

She laughed. "Is that comfy?"

Eyes closed, smile widening, he chuckled. "Not really."

"Which one was it tonight?"

She was talking about the bedtime story. Gary grinned. "Which do you think?"

"The caterpillar?"

"The caterpillar." He opened his eyes and looked at the TV, playing one of Aissa's favourite game shows. "Is that bloke still being a dick?"

"Yep. Blaming the whole team because he didn't know the capital of Denmark."

"You're going to hate me…"

"Please tell me you're joking."

He chuckled. "I've never been much good at geography."

"It's Copenhagen. And I could never hate you."

He was about to reply when his phone rang from the coffee table. He moved suddenly towards it, almost knocking Aissa's hot chocolate out of her hand. It had been the same ever since Scott told him what was happening in his marriage: waiting for the next call. Gary wasn't sure if *he* could call Scott, what the consequences would be for his friend.

Unlike the other times, it *was* Scott. He answered quickly. "Mate."

"All right, Gary?" He didn't sound like Scott at all. There was none of the usual confidence, no bantering note in his voice. "I hope I'm not interrupting."

"Never. Give me a sec." Gesturing to Aissa, Gary took the call into the next room, walking quietly so he didn't wake the children. He went into the garden and closed the door behind him, the spring air bracing. "I'm glad you rang. I've been waiting to hear from you. I've felt so damn useless, but I didn't know if I *should* call."

"You made the right decision," Scott said. "If you rang and she was there… I don't know what she'd do. But it wouldn't be good."

"Is it safe to talk?" This conversation didn't match with the swing set at the end of the garden, the trampoline sitting next to it. "This is going to sound nuts, but is this–"

"A secure connection?" Some of Scott's old, well, *Scottness* returned to his voice. "She's out for the evening."

They paused. It was difficult to know how to talk to him. Usually they slipped into the easy banter they'd started in university together. A cold breeze blew through the garden, against Gary's bad hip, and he was reminded all over again of why he had to do everything to help his friend.

"Scott?" Gary said finally.

"I'm here." Scott was crying; Gary had never heard him like this before, and he found himself struggling to think of something to say. "I can't take this. It's non-stop. It's never going to end. When all the money's gone, when all my bloody dignity's gone... and even then she won't stop. She's never going to stop. Maybe it's time."

A chill touched Gary's spine. He should've done more. He'd kill Casey if that's what it took. For Scott. For the man who'd saved his life. "You better not be saying what I think you are."

"It's hardly been three weeks," Scott went on, as though Gary hadn't spoken. "And already she's turned me into a snivelling mess. I don't even recognise myself. When I look in the mirror, it's like, like, who the *fuck* is that bloke?"

"Have you been drinking?"

The answer came with the *tsk* of a can being opened. "How do people do this? How do they live in abusive relationships, for *years*? How can that even be possible?"

"Scott–"

"I can't imagine what it does to a person. Or I can. I can and I can't. I'm not and I am. Fuck me."

"Scott..."

"The chunks it takes out of you. And the craziest part..." He paused, sipping audibly on his can. "The sickest part is thinking, right, when this is all over, when she's gone, am I going to be able to put myself back together again? And this is after *three weeks*."

"You don't have to be embarrassed. The timescale doesn't matter. You're going through hell."

"I asked her if she was Natalie's girlfriend."

"What did she say?"

More glugging, then he laughed bitterly. "Riddles. Nothing. Just like usual."

"I want to see you. But I don't want to put you in a bad position."

"Forget about me. That's the best thing you can do."

"That's the drink talking."

"Hmm."

Gary stood and paced the garden. The security light switched on and Kiki, their Chihuahua-Jack Russell cross, came bounding out of the doggie door. The black-and-tan dog waggled her tail as she ran in mad circles, grinning up at Gary.

Gary knelt, softly stroking the dog behind the ears. "Scott, mate, you need to remember who the fuck you are."

"Not this again–"

"*Yes*, this again. You're a tough bastard. That's who you are. You're the bloke who saved my life. You're strong and loyal and good. Don't you dare start losing hope on me."

"I'm not as brave as you think I am," Scott said.

"You are. I saw it."

"Anybody would've done that."

"No, they wouldn't have." Gary stood when Kiki bounded away, cocking her leg on the trampoline's base. "Can I come by the school tomorrow? I'm guessing visiting your house is off-limits. Or the pub?"

"I can't come to the pub," he said matter-of-factly. That hurt, how Scott seemed to have accepted his fate.

"School, then. We can strategise about what steps to take next. Or we can just talk for a while."

"You have to check the school isn't being watched," Scott said. "She sometimes visits, spies on me in the classroom. It's gotten me into trouble before."

Into trouble. Like he was a kid. Gary wanted to scream.

"I'll check. I'll double- and triple-check. All right, Scott? I'll see you tomorrow? I'll come by at lunchtime."

Scott sniffled. "Okay. Yeah. It'd be nice to see you."

"I'm here for you. I'm always here for you. No matter what."

"I know."

Gary tried for a laugh. "I guess you didn't see the game last night?"

"No."

"Bloody nightmare, mate. Nightmare."

Scott tried for a laugh too, but they were both faking it. They couldn't speak about anything regular when this was going on. Scott took another long sip from his can, and then there was the *crunch* as he crushed it. A moment later, there was a *tsk*.

"This is my treat," Scott said. "Eight cans because I've been a good boy. I loved this woman. At the start, when she sprang this bloody– this *trap*, I told her I still loved her. But I don't anymore. I hate her. I wish she was dead."

"So do I."

"To be honest, mate," Scott went on, his voice slurred. "I don't want you getting involved in this. You've got so much going on. You've got your kids and Aissa and a whole life... Just forget about me, mate."

"I can't do that."

"You can. Because, mate, honestly... I don't want you getting hurt."

"I'm not afraid of her."

Scott laughed bluntly. "Tell me about work. Tell me the most boring thing you can think of, something from the real world."

Gary wanted to argue, but Scott sounded desperate. So he did what his friend asked. He spoke about an account he was working on, all the mundane ins and outs of combing over the books, as Scott drank his can then opened another.

173

37

LAUREN

Every time Lauren closed her eyes, she saw the cat; she saw the crimson streaked through the fur. And then it was Casey's expression, the tedium, the vacancy.

Lauren rolled over, trying to get comfortable, and then rolled over again.

Morgan huffed from the other side of the bed. "I've got work tomorrow."

"So have I."

"Settle down then."

Lauren sighed. "I'm trying."

She wasn't sure if she should tell Morgan about everything that was happening. It was a tricky situation, meaning she'd have to venture into territory both wanted to avoid. There was no way she could describe the cat video to Morgan; it was too haunting, too cruel to inflict that on another person.

Lauren opened her eyes and looked at the bold red letters of the clock, the blood-red letters. It was almost three.

"What's wrong?" Morgan asked, back turned, face buried in the pillow.

"Just work."

"Is it about *him*?"

Lauren stifled a groan. "Are we going to have that conversation?"

"I don't like you working with him."

Lauren attempted a joke. "Jealous, are you?"

But Morgan didn't rise to it. It was probably in poor taste anyway. "You've been acting weird for almost a month. Don't think I haven't noticed. It's like you're always somewhere else, or wishing you were."

"I'd love to talk about it with you. But something tells me you don't want to hear it."

"Not if it's about him."

"Well, it is."

"Then keep it to yourself."

Lauren rose from bed and left the room, the light from the landing guiding her. Zora looked up, blinking her eyes open, and Lauren leaned down and scooped her up. Zora was the cuddliest cat Lauren had ever known, behaving like a dog sometimes, always keen to be held and stroked. She curled up in Lauren's arms as they walked downstairs.

Dropping onto the sofa, she lay with Zora still in her arms, wondering how anybody could possibly harm an animal.

How badly did a person's circuitry have to be wired to make them capable of that?

She was thinking about Markus, about the lockbox and the key. She was thinking about ending this.

Zora yawned, sprawling out on her back. Lauren tickled her belly and let her head fall, closing her eyes.

38

GARY

Gary walked down the school's hallways, paranoia touching him. He'd searched the surrounding area of the school as Scott had suggested. He'd felt like a jackass, making the circuit, looking in as many cars as possible. But Scott had asked him to do it, and so he did.

He nodded to one of the teachers as he passed. He'd visited Scott at school a few times, as well as attending a couple of their parties. Gary adjusted his visitor's badge.

Approaching Scott's classroom, he took a moment to ready himself for what he might find. Scott had sounded so different on the phone, not at all like the man Gary had known for more than a decade. It had been over a week since they'd seen each other. How much could Scott realistically change in that time?

Gary wasn't sure, but the thought made his hips ache, as if leaching onto the old memory.

He rounded the corner and walked through the door. Scott wasn't there. Instead, a woman sat at the desk.

"You must be Lauren."

She rose, covering her mouth as she swallowed her lunch. "I'm afraid you have me at a loss."

"I'm Gary." He crossed the room and offered his hand. "Is Scott about?"

She shook his hand, saying, "No, he called in sick... again."

"Fuck." He flinched, shaking his head. "Sorry. I just... did he say why?"

Gary's mind flooded with a million nasty visions, all of them worse than the last. Casey could've badly hurt him and... No, that wasn't right. Scott must've called in sick himself. But what if Casey had done it for him, claiming he'd lost his voice?

"Just that he wasn't feeling well," Lauren said.

"Did you speak to him?"

"Yes."

"I mean, *him* specifically."

She nodded. "Yes."

Lauren touched her bracelet, in what seemed like a familiar gesture. "I'm not sure if I should mention this. But, well... Has Scott spoken to you recently, about anything, uh, related to his personal life?"

Gary looked at her, reading the glint in her eyes. "Yeah. He told me you'd offered to go to the book club for him."

Gary sat down and Lauren did the same. He thought he could see concern in her expression.

"I found something yesterday," Lauren said. "Scott calls you his *best friend*, sort of gets an excited little-boy look when he says it. I'm guessing he won't mind if I tell you?"

Gary found himself smiling; he liked it when people offered up light banter. It made everything easier. "So what was it?" he asked.

"I went to visit Casey's ex-husband..."

She glanced at Gary, as if silently questioning why Scott didn't ask Gary to go. And that was a good point, as far as he was concerned. He'd made it clear he would help him. But what had Scott said last night? He didn't want Gary getting involved.

"All right," Gary said.

"He showed me a video of Casey killing a cat."

Gary stared for a few moments, not really sure what to say. It was almost like he was waiting for a punchline. "Are you sure?"

"It was two minutes of her violently butchering a British Shorthair with a trowel. I'm sure."

Gary closed his eyes. He saw Casey on the wedding day. Despite his concerns, Gary had gone as his best man and had a fantastic time. As she and Scott were standing at the altar, he truly believed it for a little while; they were going to work. They were too in love *not* to work.

"We need that video," Gary said.

"But how? Markus threw me out when I asked for it."

"I don't care how. But we need to get our hands on it. We can't let this happen. Scott said something last night, about not wanting me involved. But fuck that. I have to be. We need that video. We need to make her stop."

Lauren sat up. "I want that too. But how?"

"I don't know. But there has to be a way. I won't let this lunatic ruin him. That man saved my life, saved my goddamn life, and now she's, she's..." Gary trailed off, picking at the desk, splinters biting into his thumb. "I can't let it happen."

"Scott saved your life?"

"He's never mentioned it?"

"Until recently, we didn't talk about personal stuff."

"It was when we were in university. We were in our second year, so that makes us nineteen, twenty. Anyway, we were at a club and I got chatting to a girl. Things were going well, I thought. We were hitting it off. She asked me if I could go across the street and get her some cigarettes. Weird request, I thought, but screw it... Not to be blunt–"

"But you thought you were going to fuck her."

Gary laughed. "Yeah, pretty much."

Lauren smirked. "And then what happened?"

"It turned out she was luring me outside so her friends could jump me. I'd withdrawn three hundred in cash for the night, like a moron, and I was also flashing it around... like an even bigger moron. I should've given them the money, but I was drunk and pissed off and I swung on one of the bastards. That was a mistake. There were five of them, and they started kicking the shit out of me. I thought I was going to die. My hip and my leg still give me trouble from it. One of them kicked me so hard I was sure I'd never walk again."

Lauren covered her mouth.

Gary continued, feeling a violent shudder inside of him, even now; he'd taken on a kind of monotone voice, the way he always did when he told this story. "A crowd had gathered, but nobody was getting involved. These were proper nutcases. One of them kept screaming that he had a knife. Everybody was drunk and scared. Then I blacked out. Scott told me later the bloke shouting about the knife had taken a running start and kicked me in the head.

"When I woke up – it was only a few seconds later, I think – Scott was there. He pushed through the crowd and he roared, Lauren, *roared* at them. He wasn't scared. He charged at them and he swung like a madman. The fighting was vicious. One of them bit his pinkie finger off, spat it into a drain. It was mayhem."

Gary had been drunk and this had all happened years ago, but he'd never forget the way Scott cried out when that savage spat blood and flesh into the gutter.

"But Scott wouldn't stop. He went berserk. Eventually they were forced to back off. By then there were sirens in the air. Scott knelt at my side and checked over my injuries. We'd both done first aid, mostly because it looked good on the CV. He didn't care that he was bleeding from a dozen places himself. When I woke up in the hospital – three days later – Scott was there, a bandage on his hand and a smile on his face."

Gary was trembling with the force of the memory. "Without him, those pricks would've beaten me to death."

"I've got an idea," Lauren said. "A way to save him, like he saved you. But I'm not sure you'll like it."

Gary was about to ask what, then he noticed a small cross hanging from the desk lamp. The sight was so unexpected, he had to ask. "Is that yours?"

Lauren smiled tightly. "No, it's Scott's. I'm not sure if I should move it. I'm pretty sure there's a rule about religion in the classroom."

"Scott isn't religious," Gary said. "His mum was, but nothing major. And I know he isn't a fan of Natalie's parents, the way they look down on people because of their religion."

"He brought it in a few days ago."

"I'm sorry. This is like finding out he goes to sex clubs or something." Gary laughed, shaking his head.

"Maybe it's helping him through this," Lauren said softly, and Gary felt like a dick.

"Yeah, maybe," he said. "But I don't want there to be any *this*. Put that away, Lauren, just in case."

"Do you think so?"

"What if one of the kids tells their parents this school – that has no religious affiliation at all – is displaying a cross in the classroom? I'm not saying it's a big deal. But these days... I want Scott to have a job to come back to. He'd want us to move it."

"All right." Lauren unwrapped the small cross from the lamp and put it in the drawer. "So do you want to hear my plan?"

39

SCOTT

"Dance, you beautiful boy, dance!"

Scott had been doing just that for what felt like hours. Casey was sitting in the armchair, drinking directly from an expensive bottle of wine. She'd delighted in telling him this bottle had cost over a thousand pounds, casually pouring some on the floor as she said it.

He wasn't a good dancer, never had been. He moved around the room just enough so she didn't bring her hand down on her phone. She'd opened her email application, bringing up the draft, the message that could end his life.

With one tap, she'd told him, "It will all come crashing down."

Scott was noticing something about his wife: something that made him wonder where she could possibly take this next. She was growing tired of the games. Even her smiles, when he really studied them, seemed forced; it was like she was play-acting her sadism, the same way she'd pretended during their whole relationship.

A familiar surreal note touched him. This was his life,

dancing awkwardly so his wife didn't ruin him. He spun from one side of the room to the other, his legs aching, feet throbbing.

Casey clapped her hand against the bottle, her rings making a *tap-tap-tap* sound against the glass. But there was something off about the gesture. Again Scott intuited she wasn't enjoying this. It was more like she thought she should have been. It reminded Scott of the times he'd attended plays with Natalie, clapping enthusiastically for her sake even if he'd found the performance boring.

But who was Casey performing for? Herself?

It wasn't like *he'd* complain if she stopped.

After taking another swig, Casey sat forwards. "On your knees. Now."

Scott's instinct was to immediately obey. He remembered the pulsing agony of the Aga's heat against his hand, the shame of Casey mounting him, of her moaning in his ear, of his own tangled grunts in the last moments. It was all too much.

He couldn't do this anymore; it wasn't like the long breaths punctuated by quick pain underwater. This was just drowning.

"No."

Now she looked interested. "No?"

He stared at her as steadily as he was able. Which, admittedly, wasn't impressive at all. He could only hold her gaze for a second. "Stop it, Casey. Just stop it."

"This is your grand plan, is it?" Placing the wine bottle on the floor, she stood and walked over to him. "After all you've *made* me do, your big plan is to say no. And I suppose this is the part where I respect your bravery, where I develop a new admiration for you? Maybe you've been thinking all you need to do is show me you're not afraid, you've had enough."

Reaching up, she tenderly trailed her fingernails down his cheek. "The problem is, Scottie dear, I can see how terrified you are in every single look, in every bead of sweat on your forehead.

I can smell it, even. Big tough man, big strong man Scott, scared of a tiny little woman."

The words hurt him somewhere deep, somewhere ignored.

He groaned, thinking of the other games: handcuffing himself to the bed, what came after, as she stared dead-eyed down at him. "Surely this is enough."

She moved her hand to his neck, tightened her squeeze, not enough to cause him pain. Not yet. "It's enough when I say it's enough."

"You're not even enjoying it."

She flinched. Her nails dug deeper. "How the *fuck* would you know what I do and don't enjoy? You know nothing about women, and you certainly didn't know a thing about me. You *don't* know a thing."

Her grip tightened and tightened; Scott suppressed a scream.

"Am I wrong?" he asked, voice tremoring.

Her hand began to close, fingernails digging into his skin with such vicious force Scott was sure she was going to draw blood.

"Yes, you're a thousand, a million times wrong. This is the cleverest, most satisfying thing I've ever done. It's proof I'm better than everybody else. So many people tried to make me feel small, my pervert dad and my weasel husband and, and, and *everybody*. It's always been the whole world against me. But nobody understands what I'm capable of. Nobody understands how impressive I am."

Her words were empty air. Scott stared at her.

Casey huffed. "On your knees. Don't make me ask again."

"No. I'm done. This has to end. Take all my money. Have the bloody house if you want. Have the car. Have everything. Just let me go."

"I have to say – and I hope you don't take offence, truly, I do

– but you really are one dumb piece of fucking shit. As if begging is going to work. You should do something."

It wasn't the first time she'd said something like that, with the same intensity, the same implication. "I'd never hit a woman."

She grinned. "Oh, but you would."

"You're wrong."

"Fantasy and reality, Scottie, there isn't much of a line there. I think that's from Shakespeare. I told you I was clever. Anyway, I've got something to show you."

She returned to the chair, scooping up her phone. Scott did his best to hide the tension which seized him, which always seized him when she touched her mobile.

She swiped and tapped, then showed him the screen.

Beth Vaughn sat in Scott's living room; that explained one of her recent absences. Her eyes were bloodshot and her make-up streaked down her cheeks. She looked like a terrified teenage girl. She looked convincing.

"This is a hard video to make. I don't even know where to start. Like, how can I explain what he did to me without breaking down? But I have to get this out there. I can't let him hurt anybody else." She took a moment, gathering her courage. Scott could imagine parents all over the country, the world watching this. Pitying her. Hating him. "My history teacher raped me."

Casey paused the video. "Seen enough?"

"That poor girl has nothing to do with this."

"That *poor girl* was paid generously for her work. It was more than anybody ever did for me. She's smart; I think she'll do well. But I bet you look down on her."

Casey released her hand. Scott moved away, touching his raw skin.

"Don't you?" she snapped. "You see her as the future

sludge of society, just another stupid kid who'll marry a stupid man and get a stupid job that's oh-so beneath the likes of you."

"No." It wasn't true. "I want to help her."

"You are. At least, your dead daddy is. Don't worry about her. You know what to do."

Scott wanted to be strong. He wanted to be like that young man who'd charged into the fray to stop those bastards from beating up his friend.

"You have *nothing*," Casey said. "No way to stop me. Knees. Now. On your fucking knees."

She scooped up her bottle and moved over, raising her other hand. "Fucking *knees*. Knees, Scott. On your knees, you sick fuck."

He fell to his knees and looked up at his wife; there was no choice. His eyes stung with tears. "Now... now what?"

"Don't flinch, okay, baby?"

She poured the contents of the wine bottle over his head. The red wine streamed through his hair, down his neck, tickling down his spine. He detached; he became a statue, inside and out, dead, rock, nothing. She huffed and tossed the bottle at the wall. Scott remained still even as it shattered.

"So obedient," she said. "I'm going out."

Scott didn't ask where. He could only hope she stayed out for a few hours, giving him a chance to recover and get ready for the next round.

Casey paused at the door. "You need to know something. You can dream things into existence. There are so many things that are true, if you believe them, if you honestly give yourself to them."

She'd been saying similar things for days, and like usual, Scott had no clue what she meant; it was just another of her crazed rants. Like the night before when she'd said she was going to be a pop star. He couldn't tell if she believed it in the moment, was faking it, or if it was something in between.

A reverberation moved through the house when she slammed the door. Scott waited until he heard her car screech from the driveway, and then he fell onto his side and drew his knees up.

The tightness came, in his chest, his head getting fuzzy as he struggled to draw in enough breath.

He wrapped his arms around himself, imagining they were Natalie's. He didn't care if she wanted to leave, to be with her girlfriend instead; he didn't even care about the complicated corners of their marriage. As long as they could remain friends. As long as she'd let him press his body against hers, not in a sexual way, but for the warmth, the promise, the lie that he'd escape this misery.

40

NATALIE

As well as fear, as well as violence, Scott would use money to manipulate me. This part pains me so much, especially because I was earning more than him for most of our marriage. But somehow he gained control of our finances.

No, not *somehow*.

He turned feral and attacked me one evening, wrestling my purse from me and tearing out my bank cards. Waving them in my face – he was so malformed with rage – he ranted about what a slut I was. I was using my bank card to meet men in hotels; I was a whore, I was cheating on him, I was defective, not the wife he deserved.

It was all so pathetically familiar by then. I was able to retreat far back into my mind, nestled in my private prison, watching it all unfold. Next came the predictable, with his hands on my body, his tongue dragging roughly up my cheek. I remember thinking of the dog we never had. Scott had flatly refused every time I suggested a furry companion might make our home life a little less...

And then I'd trailed off. He'd snapped his gaze to me, eyes narrowing.

"A little less *what?*"

I'd shrunk away from him. There was another night: one of our so-called good evenings, meaning he hadn't hit me, and I wanted to keep it that way. Shaking my head, I looked down at my book. It was a miracle he was even allowing me to work on my creative writing course in bed with him. A few days earlier, he'd hit me bad, so maybe this was his deranged way of apologising.

I had to take a break. Anyway...

My creative writing teacher was a radical woman, a hippie who'd had a series of poetry books published in the nineties, and more recently a children's fantasy series. She was intense and believed in taking what she called *alternate paths* to develop one's writing ability.

"My father believed in *method writing,*" she'd explained to the class once. "He'd lock himself in his office at the back of the garden any time he was working. He explained to me how it worked. His entire mental landscape would become the narrative, the characters, the world of the story. He'd lose his sense of self, only seeing another person when my mum brought him his meals. Sounds insane, yes?"

The class laughed uneasily. She looked like she was about to launch into another of her diatribes.

"He went on to write nine bestsellers. Many of you know his name. He sadly passed when he was only fifty-two. It was a few days before my name first appeared in print. It's one of life's unfunny jokes."

The teacher had given us an assignment, something daring and strange, and I knew working on it in bed was a mistake. If Scott got his hands on it...

I'm not sure where to go from here. How can I explain how tragic and helpless I felt any time I had to ask to borrow one of the cards, *my* cards, so I could buy something at the shop? How can I explain the agony of wincing every time my husband walked past the bathroom door, the floorboards creaking, then pausing, my eyes fixated on the door handle?

Don't turn, don't turn.

I had married a young man with a soul full of hope and love, who I believed would always protect me. He'd never let anything bad happen to me. And he'd certainly never become the bad thing himself.

I'm not perfect. I lied to my husband for years; I never plan on telling him the truth. I may have to look through these entries when I'm done, cutting out all the parts about me and my lover, the woman who captivates my thoughts whenever I'm not with her, the name carved into the wall near the gnarled wind-battered tree.

Or maybe...

Can I mix in some realness with all the hurt?

They say actors draw on what they know. I'm sure it's the same with writers.

I would love to say life got better. Scott realised he'd become a monster and he enrolled in therapy, taking it seriously, addressing whatever demons were haunting him. His childhood, as far as I knew, had been happy enough. He had a good relationship with his mother, who lived on the other side of the country. There was nothing to explain the ogre behind his charming smile. He'd never said a single word about his dad, other than he loved him. That was it.

I'm tired, my eyes growing heavy. I've been writing for three and a half hours and my hand is beginning to cramp. My mouth is dry. That's the beautiful thing about writing, how it can consume a person, make them forget the rest of the world exists.

I'm rambling now. I think I'm getting addicted to the feeling of the pen against the paper. The library is so quiet. Except for the occasional bird chirping from the greenery outside, there's nothing, just me and the page.

41

LAUREN

The entranceway of Scott's house was a mess of cardboard boxes, towers of them stacked on top of each other. Some of them weren't open; others spilled out packing material across the floor.

As Gary led her into the dining room, they passed dozens of expensive-looking purchases, TVs and hair straighteners and bottles of wine casually strewn across the carpet. There was an exercise machine awkwardly wedged against the wall, with a designer handbag at its feet, the logo smeared with what looked like tomato sauce. Or Lauren hoped it was.

Scott sat at the kitchen table. He looked like a corpse. The counters were covered in more boxes. A coffee machine gleamed from the corner, with a blender sitting next to it, the cord still wrapped in its protective tape.

"Afternoon," Scott said. "Welcome to my lovely home."

Gary sat next to him. "How long have we got?"

Gary had sneaked in through the back, checking if Casey was around, before coming out and waving Lauren inside. Part of Lauren hoped they ran into the cat-killing bitch.

"No idea," Scott said. "Sometimes she'll go out all night.

She's a drug addict on top of everything else. She showed me her stash a couple of nights ago. She's got everything in there, weed and coke and pills and shrooms and even a couple of needles. We talked about drugs in the beginning, you know, and she said she'd never touch them."

Scott took a long sip of his coffee, staring straight ahead, as though he was talking to himself. Lauren quietly sat opposite the two men.

She found her hand straying to the bracelet, as it often did.

"How much has she taken?" Gary asked.

"Almost all of it. I've got a few grand left."

Scott was still talking in that disjointed way, as though he wasn't present. Lauren wished she could comfort him, even if she knew there was a chance he was as bad as Casey.

Gary looked at Lauren, expression tight. Lauren knew what he meant. Scott was gone, floating someplace faraway, barely aware they were there.

"We're here to talk about how we can end this," Lauren said.

Scott finally looked at her. "Don't say that unless you mean it."

"Your settings are private on Facebook, right?"

Scott nodded.

"And your profile photo doesn't show your face."

"It's a photo of the horizon, from..."

Lauren knew: the wedding.

"I need to be careful with social media. My job." He laughed, and then it turned into a violent cough. He battered his chest with his fist, grinning manically. "My job, it'd be at risk if I put the wrong stuff out there on social media. Plus I don't want the kids to be able to find me. My job. I've let her torture me for my job."

"Mate." Gary frowned. "It's going to be all right. You know that, don't you?"

Scott stared. "Do you want to see something?"

Before they could answer, Scott took his phone from his pocket, tapped a few times, and then slid it to the edge of the table so Lauren and Gary could watch at the same time. Beth Vaughn appeared and began to explain, in detail, how Scott had raped her.

"That's what I'll be," Scott said, over the sound of Beth's voice. "Not just a bloke whose nudes got leaked. Not just an embarrassment. I'll be a rapist too, a child abuser. Even if there's no proof, nobody will ever want me around their kids again. Casey told me she's added it to her email draft. At midnight, *poof*, my life goes. *Poof-poof-poof.*"

With each word, he chipped at the table with his fingernail.

"We've got a way to make her stop," Gary said. "But I didn't want to go ahead without your permission."

Lauren sensed Scott was searching for a way to exert control, and this was the only thing he had mastery over, his thumbnail scraping across the wood, pieces flaking away. Casey had stolen everything else. She'd even stolen his dignity, his fight. He didn't look like the man Lauren had worked with at the school for so many months.

"Scott," Gary snapped. "Did you hear me?"

"Why would you need my permission?"

Lauren rested her forearms on the table. "Because what we're planning... it's not exactly legal."

42

SCOTT

"They're going to get suspicious if I keep calling in sick." Scott placed his phone on the bed, looking across the room. Casey was perched on the chair at the vanity unit, dabbing her face with a make-up brush. "I've worked there for years and only called in sick a couple of times."

"I wonder what would make them angrier," Casey said, brushing her thumb along her eyebrow and flicking something away, "pulling a sickie or raping one of your students."

"Stop saying that."

Casey grinned, looking at him. "Or..."

Scott hugged his hands tighter around his knees. He'd only woken because Casey had shouted at him. He'd wanted to sink into the mattress, into his dreams. It was difficult to remember, but he was almost certain Natalie had been there, that shy smile on her face, her eyes turned down; it was from the beginning.

And the earth was without form, and void; and darkness was upon the face of the deep. Scott had been reading the Bible through an app on his phone. He wasn't sure why; he tried to think of Natalie's pain, her parents. But the words drew him back. He was a husk, formless, with no light even in his deepest parts. He needed to be remade. He couldn't go on like this: not just this situation, but as this person. He wanted to be somebody else.

He thought of his mother, smiling down at him, sunlight beaming through high glass windows behind her.

"Where are you going?" Scott asked numbly.

"I'm not sure. I've got money to burn and all the time in the world. Maybe I'll go shopping. Maybe I'll go to the spa."

"Do you enjoy it?" Scott asked.

She turned to him, her movements fiercer this time. Her veneer dropped and her lip curled. Scott cringed, despite the distance between them. He knew how easily she could launch into one of her assaults when that look came.

"Why do you ask?" she said a moment later.

"No reason."

"You're wrong," Casey snapped.

"I didn't say anything."

"You are fucking *wrong*. I've been waiting a whole year for this. Putting up with you. Listening to you babble about the most boring pointless things. It was all leading up to this."

"You sound like you're trying to convince yourself."

She screamed as she threw the make-up brush. It smashed into the wall and then she was on him, her fingernails scraping down his neck, raking across his cheeks. She spat and hissed and elbowed him in the face before Scott managed to get his hands on her wrists, pinning her to the bed.

He shook her. "Stop it, just *stop it*."

"Do it. You know you want to. Make me pay. Hurt me, Scottie boy, hurt me badly."

Scott tightened his grip on her wrists. She didn't look bored anymore. The glint was in her eyes: the same one which had shone on their anniversary.

"You know you want to," Casey whispered.

Scott squeezed even harder, feeling her bones through her flesh. But she wasn't giving him the reaction he wanted. There was no fear; there was nothing like she'd inflicted on him. There was no release. He just felt soiled by the whole thing.

She ran her tongue over her lips. "This is the first time I've ever found you attractive."

"Because you're insane. Because you're a lunatic. Because you're a *joke*."

"You could always kill me," she mused, unfazed. "And then, at midnight…"

Scott shoved her wrists harder into the mattress.

"I'll give you one free shot." Casey turned her face sideways, presenting her cheek, the make-up smeared here and there, not properly applied yet. She was in two halves. "No consequences. No games. No emails."

"You're a liar."

"That sounds like you want to do it, Scottie dearest."

He wanted to tell her he'd never stoop that low. But he couldn't.

Letting her go, he backed away to the window, hands raised in case she sprung at him again.

She sighed as she rose to her feet. "You're so disappointing. I'm going to spend the day thinking of ways to punish you. It will give you something to look forward to."

Scott returned to bed and Casey returned to her vanity unit.

It was like nothing had ever happened, except for the stinging cuts on Scott's neck and face, the pulsing in his chest.

If somebody had been watching them, they never would've guessed they'd just had a fight. It was becoming depressingly routine. Casey attacked him – or hurt him in some other way – and then they went on with whatever they were doing.

Casey finally stood, brushing down her designer jacket, beaming at Scott from the end of the bed. "How do I look?"

"Beautiful, as always."

Physically, she'd never been more stunning. Her hair was always immaculately styled and she wore a new outfit every day. Her make-up – if she didn't attack him halfway through applying it – highlighted all her best features. But Scott found her ugly.

Before leaving, she went through her regular routine of threatening him, telling him to stay home, reminding him of the power she held over him. Scott barely heard it. He was looking at her, but not seeing her, not seeing anything.

Even his cuts didn't hurt anymore, throbbing distantly.

Scott pulled the covers over himself once she was gone, burying his face in his pillow. He willed the dream to return, for Natalie to come back to him.

Gary and Lauren were going to try their plan, but Scott didn't feel much of anything about it. Maybe it would work; maybe it wouldn't.

It didn't matter when the blackout curtains kept the room dark, when all he had to do was lie there, eyes stubbornly shut, ignoring his bladder each time it willed him to his feet.

He was putting his friend's life at risk. Or maybe not his life, but his freedom. They were going to commit a crime. If it worked, Scott might be able to fight back. But nothing had worked. Scott had stopped trying, stopped hoping.

Lying there, forgetting – or trying to – that was enough.

Such a snivelling little nobody. Such a little baby.

Eventually he had to get up. His belly was aching with the need to piss. He dragged his tired, sore body across the room towards the bathroom, stepping on countless pieces of designer clothing, each one discarded every time it was worn.

How long had it been since Gary and Lauren were there? A few days ago, he thought: three or four. They had to wait for a convenient time, they said, and he needed to hold in there; he had to stay strong.

Stay strong, but Scott's strength had already left.

He stood at the toilet, staring down into the bowl, thoughts flitting unwillingly to the previous night. He'd taken a piss in the dark and Casey had inspected it. He'd got some on the rim, apparently, so Casey had forced him to lick it.

He flushed the toilet, looking at the rim, checking it was clean.

His fists clenched. He shouldn't have to check the toilet rim was spotless. He shouldn't flinch every time the house creaked. He shouldn't have to feel like less of a man, or not even a man, because of the things Casey did to him.

He looked in the mirror, disgusted with what he found. His hair was greasy and matted. His face was covered in patchy stubble. He looked like he'd given up.

It couldn't be Scott. Scott would never allow himself to sink so easily into despair, into apathy, into whatever was gripping him. *Ebbs and flows, but never black then white, nor white then black.*

Easing into madness...

Is it sweeter?

Shouting, he smashed his fist against the reflection, splintering it. Glass bit into his palm but he didn't care. He roared and grabbed the unit, yanking it away from the wall and throwing it across the room. Plastic and glass erupted, and then Scott was in the bedroom, picking up handfuls of clothes, tearing everything to pieces.

How much was this one? A hundred pounds, a thousand?

He tore it and threw the remains onto the bed. He scooped up big handfuls and ran into the bathroom, not caring when the glass stabbed into his bare feet. He threw them down the toilet, flushed the chain, watching as the water rose and spilled over the edge.

Back into the bedroom, he began punching the TV. It was one of Casey's expensive ones. He punched until his fist bled and then turned to her vanity unit, only realising he was crying when the sounds of his sobs hit his ears.

He grabbed her vanity unit and spun, gripping it so hard splinters flaked away in his palms. His back gave a twinge as it crashed into the wall, one of the legs snapping away.

Collapsing to his knees, he bowed his head, his chest heaving.

He stayed like that for a long time, and then, once his breathing had slowed and the haze had cleared from his thoughts, he realised he needed to fix it.

If Casey discovered he'd destroyed her new vanity unit, her pride and joy, one of the only absurdly expensive items she actually *used*...

Scott looked at the clock. It was already two in the afternoon. He'd spent half the day lying in bed, not even sleeping.

"Idiot," he chided himself. "Fuck's sake."

He knelt next to the unit. It was only the leg that had snapped off, but there was some structural damage to one of the drawers. From the angle the unit had fallen at, Scott was able to see the underside of the drawer.

He was able to see a notebook, held in place with four strips of duct tape.

Scott grabbed it, even as he knew his punishment would be much worse if he added snooping to his list of crimes.

But this was too good to ignore. A notebook, maybe giving him something he could use against her?

He stripped away the duct tape, making a mental note of the book's position so he could replace it as precisely as possible.

Opening the book, he stared down at the first page, at Natalie's handwriting. These were her big bold letters, her pen flicks that sometimes spanned two lines. There was no mistaking it.

Had Casey *copied* Natalie's handwriting? Or had Natalie given away her diary before her suicide?

Scott's thoughts whirled as he read the first line.

When Scott and I met at university, we both wanted to be writers…

43

CASEY

Casey wasn't sure how long she'd been gazing down at the water. She felt certain it was staring back at her, eyes hidden in the depths. Perhaps they were her father's, dear Daddy and his dead dick and the devilish delectation he took in devouring her... And then her thoughts strayed, and she couldn't remember what she'd been thinking about.

The water, the water and the weed. She'd bought a pack of pre-rolls from her dealer, ten different strains, and then unrolled them and emptied them into one big bag. Shaking them together, she'd created a lucky-dip medley, with mind-stimulating sativa mixing with body-calming indica and everything in between.

She blinked, rubbing her face, trying to remember why she was there.

Looking around the park, she saw the school beyond the trees.

That was it; she was there to see her daughter.

She turned from the pond and walked down the lane. There was one thing she *couldn't* forget, no matter how hard she tried, and that was the way Scottie had behaved that morning. It was like he'd seen right into her, into her heart, her soul, her whatever-the-fuck-it-was. He'd looked deep and picked at her most sensitive spot.

"You sound like you're trying to convince yourself."

"Pardon?"

Casey looked at the voice, the owner of the voice. An older man with a dirty buttoned-up jacket and muddy jeans and an ugly mutt sitting at his feet. The dog was small and rattish, with beady eyes and crust all around them. The little bastard growled as Casey stared down at it.

"I didn't say anything," she told the man. "And please, shut your fucking dog up."

He gawped. The rat dog let out a yap.

"Are you all right?" the man asked.

"Fuck you."

Casey walked ahead. Stopping at the park gate, she looked across the road at the school. Class hadn't finished yet. Casey sat on a bench and took out a fat blunt, so big she'd hardly been able to close the paper. The pre-rolls had come with dusty weed, so she sprinkled it, remembering when she was a girl and she'd been fascinated with glitter.

And *he* told her she was beautiful. *He* said glitter made her a woman. *He* had squealed like a piggy when she pushed the iron against his meagre maggot.

As she lit and inhaled, her mind felt like it was falling down a wormhole. She held the smoke and blew it out slowly, not allowing herself to cough. But there was no high, no elation, no humour. Everything was *flat*.

She inhaled, inhaled some more, kept pulling on the blunt until the end crisped down to halfway. All that green heaven in her lungs, but there was nothing as she blew it out. She remembered the first time she'd smoked, with her dad and his friend, at the back of the garden. And then Dad had leaned over and, right in front of his friend... and nobody cared. Nobody *thought* to care.

Somehow, the blunt had vanished. She'd smoked it down. She could hardly remember. She was so tired of feeling this way. She longed for that moment, the point when she'd told Scott about her plan. It had been perfect, everything as she'd arranged it, as though she was dreaming reality into being. She'd done it, once again, proven how much better she was.

Standing, she looked down at herself. Sometimes weed made her forget about her appearance, almost convinced her she was a scrawny girl again, her tights soaked in piss because she'd stupidly thought avoiding the toilet meant avoiding *him*.

"Him, him, him," she said, thinking of Markus, of her father, of Scott, all of them useless and nothingy and hateful.

She turned, closing her eyes for a moment, steadying herself. She was getting all the physical side effects, sluggish and cloudy, without any of the mental clarity that normally came along with it. She'd left her treasure trove in the car's glovebox; maybe she should go back.

But she was there for a reason.

That was it. Polly.

Her daughter was called Polly. That was so embarrassing she almost screamed. She sounded like a child's toy or a pet.

She approached the school gates, taking out her phone and glancing at it. It was nearly three. That surely meant the children would be coming out soon. Casey wasn't sure what time her daughter finished school; she only knew this *was* her school because she'd followed Markus a few times, just in case she needed access to her daughter.

Somebody approached, a woman who had way too many teeth. She looked like a fucking donkey. How could somebody show so many teeth while frowning?

"Hello, can I help you?" she asked, walking through the open gate.

"What?" Casey snapped.

The woman raised her hands. Casey tried to remember she had to pretend. She had to turn on the charm.

"Learned that skill from dear dead Daddy," she told the donkey-toothed bitch.

"Excuse me?" The woman was trying to play the concerned citizen; Casey could already hear her bragging to her friends about the situation, about how well she'd handled it. *There was this crazy lady outside school...*

"Who are you?" Casey demanded.

"My name's Judith. I'm a TA here. One of the parents mentioned you'd had a little exchange in the park?"

That upswing at the end of her sentence was the worst part, as if she was talking to a child.

"Have you been drinking today?"

"I'm waiting for my daughter, so kindly leave me alone."

There, that was polite, much more than she deserved. But the woman wouldn't let it go. Casey had made it clear she didn't want to talk, and yet the donkey trotted forwards anyway.

"Well... you see."

"Do I. Do I see."

"It's five o'clock. We'll be closing the gates soon. I'm only here because of cooking–"

"I didn't ask for your fucking life story." Casey thought of sitting in the park, how it had felt like no time at all. But there were no parents around, no kids; she'd been *sure* it was three.

"Who's your daughter?"

The woman was getting far too close. It looked like she was about to spring at Casey. And then maybe she'd hit her and throw her down and kick her and then drag her into a bedroom with the mattress on the floor because they couldn't afford a bed frame, no way, not with how expensive beer was and weed and don't forget cocaine, and liquor was the worst of all, mix it all together in a plastic bottle and take a sip and suddenly there's no more pain, no more anything, and she could even laugh at it... laugh and laugh and laugh.

The woman gasped, her eyes bulging, bloodshot. It took Casey a moment to realise what had happened.

The woman had forced Casey to defend herself. She had her hands on her shoulders, shoving her up against the fence. Casey's hands were around her neck, squeezing, so much stronger than anybody had ever given her credit for.

"Please." Donkey's words came out strained, her hands pawing at Casey's wrists. "Please, stop... please."

It was terrible luck. The second Casey finally started to feel something again, she was forced to stop. A man was jogging up from the school building towards the gate, a real do-gooder look about him.

Casey let the woman go and turned away. She focused on the running, on the feeling of her designer heels slamming into the concrete, of the sound they made, like rain, like fingernails against a coffin. She breathed steadily, cleanly. A person could be healthy even when they smoked and snorted and – very occasionally – injected. It simply took the right spirit.

She stopped in an alleyway, leaning against the wall, her hands on her knees. She was smiling, at least; that was progress.

Maybe this was an indicator she'd made a mistake. She'd waited a year to unleash herself on Scott, dreaming of it every night, obsessively focused on how incredible it would be.

It was too much pressure.

But just then, when she'd put that donkey slut in her place, *that* had been something. There had been a flicker. Maybe, even if it pained her, she'd have to move on from Scott. It was such a waste, though, to put in all that effort for nothing.

She sighed, letting her head fall against the brickwork, listening for sirens, for commotion, for anything. But there was only the distant honking of a car horn and the closer rumbling of traffic beyond the alleyway.

This was all Natalie's fault.

If she hadn't acted so high and mighty at the book club, Casey wouldn't even have thought to steal from her; she had no reason. But Natalie's behaviour had always seemed so fake. It was annoying, how nobody else could see it, and how Natalie would look at Casey as though she was inferior. Casey would never allow somebody to disrespect her.

She'd expected stealing it to be a little thing.

Sticking out of Natalie's rucksack when she went to the toilet. The notebook, the world of secrets, the pain and the truth.

Casey had taken it, reading all the bad things Scott had done, how casually he'd committed his sins.

There were issues, of course, but reality was little more than glued-together pieces. She was thinking of the cupboard where they kept the cleaning supplies, right at the back of it; Scott never went in there. Why hadn't she thrown it out, burned it? That's what Natalie even said she wanted: for it to be burned.

But she'd need to move it soon, just to be safe. She would remember that, just like she'd remember to reactivate the code on her phone. It was pathetic, how he hadn't even tried.

And if Casey decided to move on and seek different adventures, that left a question.

What was she going to do with Scott?

44

GARY

"This doesn't feel right." Gary looked across the street, at Markus's house, as he contemplated what they were about to do. "I've never stolen anything before. Except for Sadie Cunningham's pencil case in primary school. Does that count?"

Lauren stared at him blankly. "Do you want to call it off?"

"No. But that doesn't mean I have to pretend this is, in any way, okay."

"I suppose it's preferable to allow Casey to continue torturing your best friend."

"What's your problem?" Gary said.

Lauren tapped her fingers on the steering wheel. Gary's car was parked down the road, but he'd wanted to regroup with Lauren before they went into the house. Plus they were a few minutes early. Markus had told them to wait until half past five so he could ring his mother and confirm she'd picked Polly up from netball. Gary would've called him paranoid if Casey wasn't the girl's mother.

That was the reason Markus had forced them to wait. He didn't want anything happening while Polly was home. Thinking of his own kids, Gary couldn't blame him.

Lauren didn't answer his question, just kept tapping her fingers against the steering wheel. "It's almost time."

"What if he's googled Scott?"

Lauren shrugged. "Then we tell him Scott couldn't make it, but you're his friend and you can..." She paused. "Speak on his behalf, I guess?"

"What if he lets me introduce myself as Scott, sits us down, and *then* tells us he's googled him?"

Lauren shot Gary a sharp look. "What do you think he's going to do? You'll feel a little awkward, we'll move on, that's it."

It had been easier when he was impersonating a police officer on the phone. He didn't have to look anybody in the eye, lie directly to their face. But this was different. He felt like he was about to step onto a stage, the crowd staring unrelentingly, judging his every move.

"I hate this shit," Gary said.

"He said he'd only meet with Scott. And even that took some convincing. He thinks it's his duty to meet Scott, the man who's going through what he went through."

"I know all this."

"Do you remember where the key is?"

"On the display cabinet, left-side drawer."

"And the hard drive?"

"In a lockbox in the TV unit."

Lauren sat back, fiddling with her bracelet, which she'd been doing on and off since Gary had met her.

"Is that religious or something? You're always fondling it."

Lauren laughed, but it sounded forced. "I'm not *fondling* it. I guess it's a nervous habit."

"Why are you doing this? Whenever Scott talks about you, it's always as a colleague, that's it. But here you are, ready to break the law to help him. I told you why I'm willing to cross that line. But why are you? It makes no sense."

Lauren let go of the bracelet, eyes flitting to the clock. "Two minutes."

"You're not... are you?"

Lauren looked at him, eyes narrowed. "Scott's not really my type."

Gary held her gaze, and then it hit him. "Oh, right."

"Not a homophobe, are you?"

"No, but a few things are clicking into place now."

"Please enlighten me."

"You're a young woman, with no dog in this fight. Scott means nothing to you. But you've chosen to involve yourself anyway. Which means you have a reason."

"Yes..."

"You and Natalie were together. When she died, you decided to get close to Scott, to, I don't know, to try to figure out what happened. That's why you're willing to go through all this, because of you and Natalie."

Lauren pushed the car door open, standing up. "It won't matter if we're a minute early."

"I'm right, aren't I?" Gary followed her across the street. "That's why you're doing this."

Lauren ignored him as she walked down the lane. Gary followed, annoyed she hadn't shown him any sign, one way or the other. She knocked loudly on the door, as though taking her anger out on it, and then shot Gary a look. She all but said, *Don't mess this up.*

Gary didn't know what to do with his hands. He put them in front of him, crossing them over his middle, and then behind his back. He was figuring out if letting them hang at his sides was the best move when the door opened.

Markus stepped out. "Are you Scott?"

Gary nodded. "Markus?"

Markus spread his arms and wrapped them around Gary,

squeezing him tightly. Gary didn't know what to do. Of all the ways Markus would greet them, he hadn't anticipated a hug. He patted Markus on the back.

"Sorry." Markus let him go. "I just... well... you know what it's like, with her. Not many do."

"Yeah," Gary said, feeling lost.

"Come in, come in." Markus waved a hand. "I'll make us some tea."

"Why don't I handle that?" Lauren said, and Gary knew this was it, she was getting it out of the way early. She'd said as much when they were discussing it. Whenever one of them had a chance, they'd create a distraction and the other one would grab the lockbox and the key.

"Are you sure?" Markus asked.

"Definitely," Lauren said. "This isn't about me."

Markus shrugged. "Kitchen's just through there. I'll take mine white, two sugars."

"Same," Gary said.

Lauren walked down the hallway and Markus led Gary into the living room. There were lots of photos of Polly dotted about the place, making Gary feel like a real piece of dirt. That video was the only thing keeping Casey away from this man, from his daughter.

But what was the alternative, let her abuse Scott, go on abusing him, until he was penniless and gutless and a shell of his former self?

"I'm sorry, Scott," Markus said, looking so earnest Gary wanted to scream.

"It's okay. It's not your fault."

"I get it. It's hard to talk about."

That was especially true for Gary.

"Lauren said you wanted to meet with me," Markus went on. "I couldn't say no. In a strange way, I blame myself for letting Casey loose on the world. At least, when she was with me, I was the only one who had to suffer. My therapist says thinking like this isn't helpful. But we can't stop, can we?"

Gary wanted to punch the man in the face. There was something so self-congratulatory about his tone. Gary knew this was unfair. Casey had abused him, the same way she was abusing Scott.

Maybe Gary just wished she'd never left Markus, so, that way, Scott would never have met her. It was a cruel thing to wish on a man.

But Markus wasn't his friend; Markus hadn't saved his life. Scott had.

"No, we can't," Gary said. "But that's the nature of–"

His words were cut off by a loud crash from the kitchen.

"Oh, for goodness' sake," Lauren said, artificially loud so Markus would hear.

Markus winced. "I better go check on that."

Gary waited as Markus stood, offered a tight smile, and then left the room.

When he was alone, Gary sprung to his feet and walked over to the TV unit.

45

SCOTT

Scott wasn't sure how many times he read the entries. He sat on the floor, next to the broken vanity unit. At first the words were blurry with his tears, but at some point he stopped crying; maybe it was around the third reread. He had to go over it again and again, trying to convince himself Natalie hadn't written this, *wouldn't* write this.

They were full of lies, with some truth sprinkled in. He *had* done impressions for his dad, during the late-night dinners, but this hadn't turned him into a pretender. The football thing had never happened. And, clearly, Natalie *had* been having an affair with a woman.

But he'd never hit her. He'd never sexually assaulted her. He'd never manipulated her.

An icy tingle moved over his body when he read the line about burning her creative writing book, with that sick smile on his face: something he'd never done, *would* never do. He'd supported her in her creative writing courses, even when she enrolled in an expensive experimental class with that hippie teacher.

He remembered finding Natalie in the garden one day, her

legs crossed and her elbows rested on her knees. She was staring at the fence with such fixation Scott found himself glancing over to see what she was looking at.

Her eyes had flitted to him, as her head remained still. "I have to memorise fifty different ways to describe this fence."

Scott had laughed, shaking his head. It was another of the teacher's strange tasks. "Well, have fun."

Natalie flushed, smiling in that ironic way of hers. "I know it's crazy, but I think it's worth a try. She's a bestselling author, don't forget. She must be doing something right."

Scott had gone inside and poured Natalie a glass of orange juice. Their hands had brushed as he handed it over. Their eyes met, and he leaned in, kissing her softly on the forehead, just to be close to her, to smell her, to taste her. To melt into her.

She'd written that he'd abused her in every twisted way: he'd controlled her, hurt her, hated her.

Scott could barely get through the entries that involved their so-called sex life.

He'd never been into that extreme stuff; he remembered when Natalie got swept up in the *Fifty Shades of Grey* mania and they'd tried it, but neither of them had enjoyed it. They'd felt silly, and Scott had felt something more than that. An inability to hurt his wife, to cause her pain, even for pleasure. In hindsight, he supposed she'd done it for his benefit. But it had given him nothing.

He brought the words close to his face, studying them, trying to convince himself it wasn't Natalie's handwriting. Perhaps Casey had faked it somehow, but why? As justification for what she was doing to him?

But Casey didn't need justification. He remembered what she'd said, about dreaming reality into being, the way she'd prattle on about how her thoughts could shape the real world, all that mad crap.

Scott felt certain Natalie had written this. It wasn't just the handwriting. It was her voice, like she was speaking to him from beyond the grave.

Scott closed his eyes and saw Casey standing over his wife, a knife in her hand, brandishing it as she forced Natalie to cover the page with these fabrications. But then the image turned to mist and drifted away. It made no sense.

Except Casey enjoyed inflicting pain. It was her driving force. Her soul, if she had one, was a place of profound sadism. Everything she did was to hurt somebody else. She'd tortured her first husband for years, she'd targeted Scott, she'd killed innocent animals... all because it made her feel good.

Scott rose to his feet, the notebook clutched in his hand. Whatever was happening here, he needed to tidy this place up before Casey got home. Then he'd figure out a way to get the answers he needed.

If Casey discovered this mess... He couldn't think about the things she'd do to him. His hand throbbed, healing from the Aga, but still tender. His body was a patchwork of bruises and cuts. His heart thumped when he envisioned Casey walking into the wrecked bedroom, finding her designer clothes torn and soaked from toilet water.

He'd have to take the clothes to the bin; she wouldn't notice. She never wore the same outfit twice anyway. Then he'd figure out how to reattach the leg to the vanity unit. He was sure there was some glue downstairs, in the same cupboard as the cleaning supplies.

He turned.

Casey gripped the frame with both hands, weaving slightly, as if finding it difficult to keep her footing.

"Somebody's been a bad boy." She looked sick, eyes glassy, cheeks pale, her words coming out slurred. "Bad boy, snooping where you shouldn't. Do you know what happens to bad boys?"

Scott raised the notebook, as though it could protect him. "Please."

Casey took a few shaky steps. When she sighed, it was with resignation, like everything had been leading there: to whatever she was about to do.

"Please," she repeated, and it was like she was honestly begging even as she mocked him. "Please, please, please. Oh, Scott. I *do* love you in a way."

46

GARY

G ary opened the drawer as quietly as he could. There it was: the lockbox. He quickly took it, feeling like he was robbing a bank. When he and Scott had first met, before he had a wife and kids, he probably would've found this funny. But now his nerves were taut, his hand trembling slightly.

"I'm so sorry about this," Lauren said, speaking loud for Gary's benefit.

Markus replied, quieter, "Accidents happen. Let me get the dustpan and brush."

"Please, let me."

"It's fine—"

"Oh, sorry."

Gary imagined Lauren crowding Markus in the kitchen, purposefully getting in his way to make the delay last longer. Gary winced as the lockbox struck the drawer. He quickly tucked it under his arm and went to the display cabinet, ignoring Polly's staring eyes.

Except the key wasn't there.

Gary cursed under his breath, standing on his tiptoes to try to see the top of the cabinet; maybe he'd put it there instead.

The cabinet was too tall.

From the hallway, Gary heard a cupboard open and then close.

"Are you sure I can't do it?" Lauren said.

"It's fine. No harm done."

Gary kept searching the drawer; then another.

Fuck it. He had the lockbox. It would be easy enough to break into; he didn't need the key.

He quickly returned to his chair, tucking the box under his jacket, then winced when he saw it: the open drawer. Cursing himself silently, he moved to the drawer, leaned down and began to close it.

"What are you doing?"

Gary turned. Lauren stood at Markus's shoulder, frowning, and Markus took a step forward. He looked so tragic in that moment, so affronted, that Gary almost apologised.

But then he thought about Scott. He remembered how hopeless he'd sounded on the phone: how empty he'd been when they visited him a few days earlier.

"Scott needs this video," he said.

Markus narrowed his eyes. "I thought you were Scott."

Ah, dammit. Gary had forgotten about that part.

"He needs it," Gary repeated. "I'm sorry. But we're not leaving here without it."

"Is that a threat?" Markus snapped. "I've already explained why I can't let you have it. She'll know it came from me. Casey *never* lets things go. She'll do things you can't even imagine. She might even hurt Polly."

Gary thought of his own children, and he knew Markus had every right to attack him.

But then his hip ached; his knee pulsed. It was like a message from the past. He remembered when those drugged-up psychos had converged on him, their shoes hammering mercilessly into every part of his body. He dreamt of that hot agony for years, the pain shooting up and down his leg, his nerves cramping.

"I'm sorry, mate. I really am." Gary strode right for the door.

Markus moved to step back at first, but then he looked at Gary's jacket: at the way Gary was holding the lockbox by cradling it to his body. He yelled and looked like he might spring at Gary, but Gary stared him down...

"Please," Markus said. "You don't know what you're doing. I'll ring the police."

"You won't," Lauren said softly from the hallway, looking ill. "You'd have to explain what was on the hard drive. You'd have to tell the police about Casey. Then we'd tell *her* you'd been talking to the police."

Markus grimaced. "You really are a piece of work."

"I'm sorry." Gary made for the door. "I'm so sorry."

"I'm ringing them!" Markus yelled, his voice chasing them down the hallway. "Just you see! Just you wait!"

Gary and Lauren left the house quickly, and then Gary stopped, leaning against the wall, bracing his hands on his knees. "I can't believe we just did that."

"We had to," Lauren said. "Give it here, then."

"What? Why?" Gary stood.

"I think it's better if I do it." Lauren put her hand out. "I can give it to him at school. It's better not to–"

"It's not even open yet. I need to get some tools and crack it open. Then we'll go to Scott. Plus, he's called in sick for the past week, you told me. What makes you think tomorrow will be any different? And what point is there in waiting? I'll sort this today, right now. Go home, bust it open, then take it to Scott."

"But what if Casey's there?" Lauren asked, seeming way too weirdly keen.

"We *want* her to be there," Gary snapped. "That's the whole point. To show her what we've got."

With a melodramatic sigh, Lauren paced across the street, towards her car.

Gary looked back at Markus's house. He was standing at the front window, his arms folded. Gary met his eye, wishing there was something he could do.

There was; he could give the hard drive back.

Instead, he turned and walked down the street.

47

CASEY

Casey had no idea how she'd driven home without killing somebody. Maybe she had; maybe she'd forgotten. She vaguely recalled the stand-off outside the school, when that smug-faced woman had tried to assault her and Casey had been forced to defend herself.

Sitting outside hers and Scott's marital home – a term that meant nothing to her – she'd cracked open her treasure box and indulged shamelessly. She'd snorted several lines of that pure beautiful cocaine; she'd popped an E. She'd smoked another medley blunt. She was floating, hardly aware of what she was doing, except that *something* had to happen.

Scott had locked himself in the en suite, darting for it when she'd walked into the bedroom and found him with Natalie's notebook in his hands.

Casey pounded on the door again. She was hitting it hard, but there was no pain. She was neither happy nor sad nor angry, but she was interested: curious to see where this would lead.

She felt like the end was coming. The end of this experiment anyway, this failure. She'd learned her lesson; next time, she wouldn't wait a year. She'd find a way to get right into the fun stuff. And she *was* still capable of fun, of enjoying herself. She refused to believe otherwise.

She hit the door again.

Scott whined, "Casey, please. Just stop it."

"I'll huff and puff and blow this house down." She giggled, because she thought it was the appropriate thing to do, a way to really freak him out. Nothing was particularly funny. "Come on, little piggy. Don't make me say it. I'm so tired of saying it."

I am a rainbow fractured in space floating colours disparate never to meet.

"Do it. Send the email."

Casey laughed. *I am all the light in the fire the hottest point will be the brightest.* "You. Don't. Mean. That."

With each word, she pommelled the door.

"Did you write this?" Of course the baby was crying, a sob making his words crackle, static coming from some far-off place.

"Your wife wrote it. You abused her."

"None of this is true."

"Liar, liar, liar." Casey kicked the door with her designer heel, kicked it again. The reverberation went up her leg and her knee twinged, but there was no pain. "Lying *cunt*. Lying fucking freak. You're pathetic, Scott. A loser. Always have been, always will be. You raped your wife."

"Did you write it?"

"Enough. Come out now. Or I press the big red button. I nuke your whole weasel life. Hurry. The fuck. Up."

She reached into her jacket pocket and took out her phone. The screen was blurry. She was glad she didn't have to type in the passcode; that joke was still without a punchline.

Luckily she didn't have to open her email app. She was pretty sure she wouldn't be able to. The drugs were all mixing around inside of her, and yet they were making her feel distant too.

It was the same way she'd felt as a girl, when *he* had done what he wanted, and off she went, bye-bye, floating into the ether.

Scott opened the door. "Did Natalie... did she show you this, and you believed her?"

"It's not a question of belief when it's absolute fact."

"Did she tell you why she wrote it?"

Casey wasn't exactly sure what happened. One moment Scott was staring at her with that annoying look on his face. The next he was on the floor, blood streaming from his head, matting his hair. Casey dropped something; the back of the toilet thudded to the bathroom floor. She caught a glimpse of herself in the mirror, then turned away. She didn't relate to the woman at all; she wasn't convinced it *was* her.

"Up, up." Casey snapped her fingers. It was time to take control of this situation. "Now, Scott."

Scott rose to his feet, cradling his head. He was crying again. She was so tired of his sobbing. She was tired of all of this. Part of her wished her father had gone all the way. There was one night in particular when he'd come close to killing her, splitting her cheek wide open with his ring, her head smashing against the wall. Her world had darkened. At the time, she'd fought it. But she longed for that dark now. A release from the numbness.

But no, no, no. She couldn't let that happen. Scott would help her. He had to.

"Cuff yourself." She gestured at the bed. Scott was familiar with the command, but still he lingered. "Now. You're such a retard."

"Please."

"If you don't do what I say..." She walked right up to him; she was looking *up* at him, and yet he did nothing. "It won't be the videos. It won't be that slut Beth Vaughn. I'll murder you. I've killed before. I'll do it again."

That was a lie. Casey had never killed anybody, except for animals, which didn't count. But she would. She was ready. That might be it, the natural progression that would end this numb purgatory.

Scott obeyed. He'd cuffed himself to the bed a few times during their games. Casey had whipped him, burnt him, beaten him, all while he lay there helpless. But she'd always stopped before doing any real harm. She wouldn't make that mistake this time.

Scott took four sets of handcuffs from the bedside table. He spread his legs and leaned down, wincing as blood dripped onto the sheets. With a *click* and then another, he secured his legs.

Then he cuffed one hand to the top bedpost.

Casey handled the last one – his left wrist – as she had the other times, and stared down at him.

He was doing that spacey-eyed thing, like he wasn't there. Casey punched him in the face. He croaked, and then his eyes went vacant again. She hit him harder, even felt a flicker inside of her, along with the beautifully real physicality of his tooth against her knuckle.

She could read his expression. He thought this was like the other times. He thought she'd toy with him and then let him loose. That was why he'd agreed to cuff himself.

He'd become too accustomed to the hesitancy of her indulgence.

I will roar I will scream nobody can beat me.

"Scottie, you really are the silliest boy I've ever met. You married a stranger. You fell for some tits and ass and some dick-sucking lips. You believed every stupid thing I ever told you. And now you've just made this so much easier..."

He tensed, the bed frame rattling against the handcuffs. "Casey–"

He went on for a while, blah-blah-blahing, but Casey didn't

listen. She was starting to feel it again, the thing which had started this whole thing. She remembered the glow in her belly the first time she learned the most valuable lesson a girl could: inflicting pain was so much sweeter than receiving it.

She sorted through her make-up tools, strewn all over the place when Scott threw his tantrum. Picking up her eyebrow scissors, she returned to the bed.

Wrong side; she wanted the other hand.

Scott whined and tried to move away from her as she circled the bed. His mistake was plain in every twitch in his face. But it was too late.

She took his pinkie finger and parted the scissors, getting everything into place.

"Casey, Casey! This is too much. You can't, please. This is too far. Think about what you're doing!"

She laughed, and it was a miracle. It was real. It was the same laughter which had struck her the first night, the laughter she'd been chasing ever since.

She was alive. She was alight. This was it, the next step, the perfect step. She was going to explore herself, fully and totally, for the first time in her life.

"You did this to yourself," she whispered, closing the scissors until they must've tickled his finger. "I didn't force you to cuff yourself to the bed." She giggled. "You *cuffed yourself to the bed*. You are so stupid."

"I didn't think– Please, let's play one of the other games, one of the other–"

A simple motion, and Scottie started screaming.

48

LAUREN

Lauren realised how stupid her plan had been. She was beginning to wonder if she'd ever actually intended to go through with it. She had been planning to take the hard drive for herself, no matter who got their hands on it first. To steal it from Gary, if that's what it took.

Then use it to confront Scott.

She'd force Scott to tell her the truth about what he did to Natalie. Lauren needed to know; the video would work. It was the only thing that could save him. He'd tell Lauren his secrets as long as Casey kept hers.

But in the end, social awkwardness had won. It was such a ridiculous thing, snatching it out of Gary's hand. She hadn't properly thought about how he'd look at her, how bizarre it would feel.

It had been about forty minutes, circling back to Gary's house then coming here. Gary was parked down the street. Lauren parked and walked over to him. He was sitting in the driver's seat, a laptop propped on the steering wheel, the hard drive plugged in and the cat video playing; the lockbox lay destroyed on the passenger seat.

He stared, his mouth open, flinching every time Casey did the terrible thing. Again and again, Casey did it, and then came the look: listless eyes, no emotion at all.

Lauren knocked on the window, her trance broken when the video ended.

"You brought your laptop."

"I had to watch it." Gary placed his laptop on the passenger seat and unplugged the hard drive. "It sounds naïve, but I never believed somebody could be... But I did; I've read books, heard stories, watched documentaries. I *knew* it, but..."

"Seeing it is different," Lauren said.

"Yeah. I kept expecting her to stop. Like she'd come to her senses. But she was conscious. I mean, it wasn't a frenzy. It was just... like an execution."

"You shouldn't have watched it," Lauren said, putting her hand out.

Gary tilted his head. "What? You want to shake my hand?"

"I thought I'd hold that so you don't end up watching it again."

"Once was enough." Gary slipped it into his jacket pocket. "Let's end this."

Lauren told herself to snatch it. She could drive away and arrange to meet Scott later. There would be nothing Gary could do, not once she was in her car.

But she didn't; she followed him down the road and up the lane to Scott's house. Maybe Scott was a good man; maybe he'd have nothing to tell. But he *would* have told, if he'd thought she could get rid of Casey for him.

Lauren looked at her bracelet, at the tree pendant, and her heart thudded.

She was in this alone now; she'd lost her support.

Gary knocked on the door.

"What are you doing?" Lauren said.

"No point being subtle." Gary hammered on the glass panes. "Scott! Casey! We need to talk to you..."

The door swung ajar, creaking as a gust of wind blew it all the way open. Lauren almost took a step back. It was like the wind had purposefully opened it. She pushed away that superstitious thought.

"Scott?" she called out, as she forced herself to walk into the house. "Scott? Are you home?"

"Scott, mate?" Gary walked in after her.

"Maybe they're out," Lauren said.

"Might as well check."

They walked around downstairs. The house was even more of a mess than last time. The living room was piled high with boxes, two layers of them stacked up against the window. There were two exercise machines and an oversized TV resting on the stand. As they searched, Lauren spotted knives, whips and paddles that looked like BDSM tools.

Gary and Lauren walked upstairs, Lauren ahead of him. She nearly stopped, asked him to go first. She pushed the idea away. There was no point being melodramatic. They had the video, the leverage, the thing that had made Casey stop. But this house was making Lauren feel like she was in a horror film.

"Scott?" Lauren walked onto the landing. Four doors were open: an office, two bedrooms, and a bathroom. There was a door at the end of the hall, the only one that was closed. Lauren walked towards it, ignoring the way her heart was thumping, telling herself to calm down.

She wondered again about being a police officer one day; maybe she could see this as a challenge. Did she have what it took, when it got right down to it, the mettle in her convictions?

Anyway, they were probably out; they'd accidentally left

their door unlocked. It happened. She'd open the door, see it was empty. Maybe she'd have another chance to get her hands on the hard drive.

"Scott?"

She pushed the door open.

Casey sprung forward and grabbed her wrist.

Lauren yelled as Casey savagely yanked on her arm, dragging her into the room. Lauren tried to balance herself.

Her vision wavered; she saw Scott, looking like he was wearing a red glove, the torn fabric trickling down his arm and the side of the bed. It was blood.

Lauren turned to find Casey locking the door.

Gary slammed against it. But too late.

"Open this fucking door!" he roared.

Casey smiled sickly. She looked like she was in the grip of an apathetic psychosis, if such a thing could exist, as though she was deriving pleasure on one level but numb on another. Lauren's thoughts were flashing, focusing on anything other than the cold fact of the scissors in Casey's hand. They were small, seeming almost ridiculous, but they glimmered red.

"They don't look very sharp," Casey said slowly, looking from the scissors to Lauren. "But they do the job."

"Casey, we have the video." Lauren would've stabbed her right then, if she'd had a weapon; she would've taken her apart piece by piece with a muddy garden trowel. "So back the *fuck* off."

In the background, Gary was worrying at the door, but this was a well-made house. The doors were thick, the locks sturdy.

Casey stared blankly for a few moments, then her lip twitched. She brushed sweaty hair from her face with the scissors; no, not sweaty. It was blood in her hair, streaks of it, making it stick together. Scott moaned from the bed.

"You mean the video Markus has," Casey said. "The little kitty cat one?"

Lauren nodded, wishing she had some way to hurt her.

Casey giggled. "You stupid dyke cunt. You think I care about that?"

Lauren gasped. She'd had words thrown at her over the years, mostly from idiots in school, but this was the most vicious anybody had been.

Casey stepped forwards, waving the scissors. "The only reason I've left Markus and Polly – *Polly*, Christ... the only reason I've left them alone is because they are the most boring and pointless people who have ever breathed. I don't care about the video."

"You're a liar," Lauren snapped. "How would you ever pretend again? How would you scam people? Your whole life would fall apart."

"So what do you want?" Casey grinned, as the door continued to rumble behind her, Gary hammering relentlessly. "You're not going to ask me to fuck you, are you?"

Casey laughed, but again her eyes were dead; she took another step forward, waving the scissors, like they were boxers feinting around a ring.

"Leave Scott alone," Lauren said.

"Do you think I'm stupid?" Casey smiled. "I looked into you, and I noticed something one day. You were visiting Natalie's grave. What a curious turn of events, I thought, my husband's work slut grieving his dead wife. I worked it all out. I used the notebook. Even if she was a *liar, liar, liar.*"

Lauren's hand flew up to cover her mouth. With each *liar*, Casey had lashed at herself with the scissors, slicing them across her belly. Thankfully the scissors didn't cut through her clothes; Casey sighed, stared at Lauren.

Lauren bumped into a heater as she moved back, shaking

her head, willing her mouth to work. "Think, Casey. You'll never be able to do this, anything like this, again."

"Oh, no," Casey said, as Gary's fist pommelled the door. "I killed a cat. What a demon I am. I feel so sorry for the poor little thing. You really are a stupid little slut, aren't you?"

Casey lashed out, looking like she intended to smash the metal handle of the scissors into Lauren's face. Lauren ducked back, shouting, just about getting out of the way. "You need to think!"

"Shut. The fuck. Up."

Casey leapt forward. The handle of the scissors hammered into the top of Lauren's skull. She felt the coldness leaking over her scalp, through her hair, seeping into it. And then it wasn't cold anymore. Lauren was on her knees, and Gary was yelling from someplace far away. Scott was even making a noise, moaning, his words even more distant than Gary's.

"Leave her alone, Casey, whatever you want to do with me, whatever with me, just leave her alone, don't hurt her..."

Casey screeched and something thudded into Lauren's head. Her eyes were heavy. She closed them and lay on the floor, her arms flat at her sides, as her heart beat in time with her skull. She hoped she wasn't dying as she went to sleep.

49

SCOTT

You tied yourself to the bed.

Scott's eyes were swimming as the pain in his hand tried to leech all his attention. The cutting hadn't gone smoothly. The scissors were sharp, but not razor-sharp, not enough to slice bone, plus they were small. She had twisted it back and forth, trying to saw it away, but she couldn't. Now his finger was mangled and his arm felt like it was on fire.

But he could lean up, just about, and see what Casey had done to Lauren. She'd struck her twice. Lauren had fallen flat. Scott was begging. He was hardly conscious of his words.

Mostly he heard Natalie's voice. Had Casey struck an artery? Was that possible, from mangling his finger?

You always were an idiot. Always scraping by. Your father was a massively successful man. But you're a mediocre secondary school teacher.

Scott was thinking of an argument they'd had once, when Natalie was drunk. She'd slapped him across the face twice; Scott had backed up, his hands raised, refusing to hit her. She'd apologised after, and that was that.

He needed to wake up, to stop letting his mind wander. "Casey, leave her alone."

"She's an idiot. She thought I cared about a silly cat video. But you don't care, do you?" She sat on the bed, stroking her hand over Scott's forehead, making him shiver and cringe at the cold clamminess. "You're not going to hate me over a silly old cat?"

"No," Scott said.

"That's good."

Gary was still hammering against the door. But Scott doubted he'd break through without an axe. He remembered hiding behind these doors; Gary was stronger than Nat had ever been, of course, but still.

"Life has never been very good for me, I'm afraid." She was speaking in a bizarre sing-song way. "My dear dead daddy did some bad things to me. But I fought back. Do you want to know what I did? Forget it. It doesn't matter what you think anyway. You did it, didn't you? You hurt Natalie."

"No," Scott whispered.

Casey smoothed her thumb down across Scott's forehead. He closed his eye, just as she began to press down, driving her thumbnail against his eyelid.

"Did you abuse Natalie, Scott?"

"I didn't, I– Ah, ah."

"Did you abuse your wife?"

"Yes, I did. I hurt her. I abused her."

"What did you do?" Casey screamed.

Her nail was driving harder; he felt like it would pierce his eyelid. "I slapped her. I punched her. I humiliated her."

Casey slowly removed the pressure. "See? That wasn't so hard, was it? I'm glad we finally have that out in the open."

Scott was dribbling and crying all over himself. He nodded pathetically. "Me too. Yes, Casey. Yes."

"I'm going to finish off this bitch. If she isn't dead already. Then we'll see what Mr Tough Guy outside wants. Sound good?"

Scott yelled at her, telling her no; he thought he did, at least. But there was so much pain and his head was rushing, as though trying to make him pass out.

He tugged at his handcuffs; he hadn't applied his three as tightly as hers, the one on his left wrist. He thought he might be able to slip out of them, but it would hurt.

"Oh, fuck," Casey said, and Gary's roaring and hammering kept going. Like a soundtrack, over and over. His friend sounded so desperate to help. "She's alive."

Scott twisted, looked. Casey was perched on top of Lauren, a big bunch of hair in her hand; the bright hair dye was showing the blood, ugly petals of it.

"What's that, sweetheart?" Casey leaned down, laughing. "No, you're not my type. But what about this?"

Casey began gouging at Lauren's chest with the scissors. Lauren let out a warble, like a dying animal, groaning in sheer pain. It was like her body was trying to make her pass out. But her agony wouldn't let her.

Scott pulled at the handcuffs, then stopped. The metal bit into his hands, even at this tightness.

He was gasping, covered in tears and snot and blood. Time had slowed down; Gary's shouting was like a drawn-out song. He heard something in the song, then his vision shimmered; he saw a smiling dog, a golden retriever, the sun shining from inside it. Then it turned, and its collar rattled: it was a cross, and the dog yapped, beckoning to Scott.

He was weeping and screaming, flitting in and out of consciousness, trying to hold the dog in place so he didn't have to think about what he was doing; the handcuffs grated his skin, pulling chunks of it away. His mangled hand screamed in agony as it collided with the metal.

Collapsing onto his side, he pulled his other hand loose; he tried his foot, but his ankle was too wide.

Such a big strong man.

Scott was weaving; the dog had gone. He'd always wanted one. Natalie had always said no.

Such a big tough guy. Do it. Do it.

Scott threw his body to the side, his legs twisting at a horrible angle. He landed halfway off the bed, stretching his body. He was upside down, clawing for Casey's arm.

Every sinew and muscle in his legs felt like it was going to snap, and then–

He heard something *crack*. He roared and then threw himself forward; his vision raged red, and he saw horns, saw a gaping mouth of red teeth. He grabbed the fucking bitch; he yanked her arm so hard it must've blown out of the socket.

She sprawled atop him, the angle awkward as he found her throat. He wasn't holding back now; Lauren was still moaning, sounding so close to the end. Scott hated himself for letting it get this far, for letting them help, for being the sort of man this could so easily happen to.

Casey was cackling as Scott choked her. He wrapped his arm tightly around her neck, pushing on the back of her head to deepen the choke; it was all instinct, the need to make her stop. He squeezed and squeezed, until she had no air for laughing; he kept going, screaming all the while, tears stinging his cheeks.

She went limp, and then Scott saw it again; he knew he'd always remember this.

The dog, sunlight, the cross.

He let her go, shuddering, weeping. Lauren was a moaning bundle on the floor.

Casey gasped, sounding groggy, then started sucking in breaths.

Scott's vision wavered.

Nat would be so jealous. She'd never been able to break that door down.

A voice – *his* voice, and he heard it, floating in the abyss of his mind, as Gary kicked the door open and rushed into the room.

50

GARY

G ary sat opposite Scott in the waiting room. It had been two days since the mayhem in the house; Gary had rushed in there and immediately pinned Casey to the floor. She had fight in her, even then, screaming, lashing at him. But he'd sat on her and rung the police.

Then, as they waited, he'd grabbed her phone and deleted all that shit. "Is this it? Do you have copies?"

Casey had only smiled, looking sick. Gary hated that he'd had to touch her.

They could only hope that was it, but Scott hadn't even asked about the emails. He was more concerned with Lauren; she'd gone unconscious again as they waited for the emergency services. The last they'd seen of her, the paramedics were wheeling her into the back of an ambulance.

Scott had sat with Gary, staring at Casey as she sang softly; that was the weirdest part, once she knew it was over. That high-pitched, soft voice, belonging to an angel, not her.

Scott sighed. He had a bandage on his finger and he was limping terribly, but he'd lied to the doctors and said it was a regular limp for him; he didn't want to take care of himself before he found out Lauren was okay.

"Casey didn't have it easy, when she was a kid," Scott said. "As she was... as we were playing her games." Scott swallowed. "She'd talk, tell me stories."

Gary snorted. "If they were real."

"You don't think so?"

"She's not exactly an honest person, mate. Maybe she had it tough, or maybe her mum and dad were good hard-working people who did their best to raise her. Either way, I'm not taking that psycho's word for anything."

"I wonder," Scott said. "But she told the truth about the email. Nothing's gone out."

Yet. Neither of them said it. They didn't have to.

"The original email account, at least. If she has another..."

"It's been more than twenty-four hours."

"She could've set it for any time. She likes that, I bet, knowing she's making me paranoid."

Gary sighed. "She's a liar. Look how she justified what she did. Those fucking diary entries. Whatever the hell that was."

Scott winced, looking around, as though the notebook was a bomb. And maybe it was. "I don't know why she would say anything like that, Gary. I swear to God I don't."

"I believe you, mate."

It was the truth; Gary knew Scott too well to ever suspect he'd do anything like that. And if it was true, why had Scott showed it to him the first chance he got? He didn't doubt his friend.

Except... well, *why* would she write that?

Scott pulled his knees up in a tentative way, wrapping his arms around them. He was constantly looking over his shoulder. "Especially since... did I ever tell you about Natalie?"

"What about her?"

Scott stared for a second, then shook his head. "Nothing."

"What, mate?"

Scott looked down at his knees, shaking his head again, almost like it was a nervous tic. "It's nothing."

"Are you saying, Natalie, did she–"

"You're not fit to say her name."

Gary and Scott turned at the voice. A woman stood at the coffee machine, her back to them. Her hair was the most noticeable thing about her: long, braided. When she turned, Gary saw she had a confident face, her features cutting. "Natalie." She blew on her coffee. "You don't deserve to say her name, neither of you."

Gary looked at Scott, but Scott was just gazing back at him. He didn't know her either.

"I'm sorry," Gary said. "I don't understand."

"Do I need to sing you a song? I was Natalie's girlfriend, and now I'm Lauren's girlfriend. And I'm going to kill you both if she doesn't wake up."

51

CASEY

Casey felt like she was sinking into a deep pit; she tried to open her eyes but they felt like they were glued shut. Her bed was ridiculously uncomfortable. She clawed her hand out, looking for the light, but instead rolled and landed painfully on the floor. She cursed, as her eyes finally opened.

She was in a cell. She could smell piss and vomit. Her lips were crusty with sick. She coughed, trying to clear her throat, but it was dry and raspy.

Snippets of a red night came to her: of screaming, cutting, laughing. She'd had the confrontation outside the school, defended herself, and then she'd gone home and... vignettes attacked her mind, vivid in their brightness, Scott screaming as she wriggled the scissors, the crunch of Lauren's delicate skull.

Yes, and then the fight with Gary...

But after, *fuck*, after she'd bragged about it to the police.

She paced the cell, shaking her head. She'd never normally let herself get so messed up on drugs; she could normally control how much she used. But she'd had some vodka before the incident outside the school. That always made them hit harder, plus there was all the smoking, all the snorting.

She hated that version of herself. What an idiot. What an amateur.

Insane ranting came to her, the words she'd flung at the police officers. *It's lucky you fucks got to me before I slit her fucking cunt throat—*

Casey winced, knowing she'd let it get out of control. The drugs. It always made her spiral. She'd make a change; she'd do it. Once she was out of here. *Would* she get out? Oh, God; this was bad. This was so, so bad. She wanted to cry.

"Here she is, Princess Charming." A slot opened in the door, light shining through a metal grille; a prison guard or police officer peered in, a spotty freak whatever he was, a real mean-looking *man*. "Any more pearls of wisdom, sweetheart?"

"I think there's been a misunderstanding," Casey said. "I don't belong here. Whatever I said last night, you can't hold that against me."

"Again with this? I can't do the same dance over and over. I've got weak knees."

He laughed at his own shit joke. Casey quickly laughed with him, but it didn't work; he only scowled.

"Don't smile at me, Princess. Twenty minutes ago, you were describing the best way to skin a child, not to put it bluntly. You went into graphic detail. A more cynical man might say you were enjoying it."

"I don't remember that."

"I know. You wake up and tell me you don't remember. We're getting your mental health assessed. Them's the rules and all that. But after what you did, I'd gladly let hungry dogs feast on you."

"You can't speak to me like that!"

Casey rushed at the door. The officer slammed the slot shut.

She pounded her fist against it, but nobody came. All she was doing was hurting her hand against the cold metal. Which meant she wasn't insane, like he was trying to say; if she was, she'd keep hitting until the door broke or her hand did. He probably had a bet with some of his dickhead guard mates. *Can we make her paranoid about her mental health?*

It wouldn't work. She sat on the bed, feeling like her skin was itching, like there were little bugs crawling over her body. She'd felt like this once before, when she was a teenager, the night she went into her parents' bedroom and hacked them to pieces with the claw end of a hammer.

But no; that was another of her fantasies, her flights into the impossible. It was how she'd survived.

Her father *had* done it. All of it was true. Nobody could tell her otherwise. Nobody could take her pain away from her. She'd earned it, through years of living in terror; she'd taken the blows and she deserved the bruises. She had her truth. She knew what had happened, who she'd been forced to become.

Which was why they were so annoying, the tears, as they flowed down her cheeks. Fantasies had sustained her, but she couldn't stop this feeling, this buzzing all over her skin.

She rushed at the door and hammered it with her fist. But again nobody came. They weren't taking this seriously. She was going to be sick. She was going to die.

That was the one true thing in her life: the night she murdered her parents with the claw end of a hammer, the nights her father invaded her bedroom, and Casey would dream. She needed to stop thinking about that stupid teenage fantasy. It was like it was trying to infect her mind: like the bugs were crawling into her brain.

That was it. Her mind was tricking her, trying to make her believe she'd slaughtered her parents and then served eight years in prison. It was trying to make her think she'd killed them because she was curious to see how it would feel, or if she *would* feel. But those were the delusions she'd entertained as a girl.

Her father *had* abused her. That was that. It didn't even make sense; she was too young to have served eight years in prison and then been married to Markus for five more. Except if she'd lied about her age. She'd remember that, wouldn't she? She'd know if she'd lied.

The bugs wouldn't stop.

She needed to be *sure*.

She stripped off her clothes, unclipped her bra and ran her fingernails over her skin. She scratched the bugs away but more of them spawned, eggs rupturing, spreading, their legs crawling everywhere. She screamed and gouged them with her fingernails.

They couldn't get to her mind. They'd make her remember the way his skull split open when the claw ruptured his forehead, the lipstick-red syrupy soup of his blood and brains. Or they'd make her think about all those nights, and the *secret girlfriend*, and the casual way he'd flaunt his abuse. She'd remember the iron, the sizzling against his worm; that wasn't part of a delusion, was it? A dream within a dream?

She was weeping and screaming, and her skin was on fire. The more she scratched, the hotter the fire burned. It purified her skin and got rid of the bugs.

Harder, she stoked the flames, as the door flew open and officers rushed in.

52

SCOTT

Scott couldn't believe he was sitting opposite Natalie's girlfriend. Morgan was right there. She'd interjected at just the right moment; Scott had been dangerously close to sharing the truth with Gary, his defences down, his emotions raw.

Gary sat beside her, aggressively chewing gum. He hadn't liked being bluntly told they had no right to speak Natalie's name, and Scott bloody agreed. He'd suffered enough over lies about his marriage.

Morgan was explaining how she and Natalie met. "We were in the drama club together at school, then she started giving me these looks, and I did it back. We didn't admit we were gay for *ages*, and then it was only to each other. But as we got older, she started getting more involved in her parents' church. She got angry with me if I ever brought it up. But she still wanted to meet in secret."

Scott stared in awe. This was his wife she was talking about, a stranger to him.

"I broke it off eventually. It was too much. But then she reached out to me one day on Facebook. I was single and thought, why not? I'm sorry, Scott."

Morgan softened, and Scott shook his head. "We went to the hangman's tree. That's where we'd spent a lot of our time as kids. Back then, the council had let it grow, bushes and grass hiding... hiding whatever we wanted to do."

"But you kept going back," Gary said.

"Yes, we did. I guess it was a special place for us."

Scott told her about the note. He had to force himself to remain quiet when she teared up. Already he was thinking about the connection between Natalie and Casey. The similarities, and what it said about him. He'd loved Natalie right until the end; he'd hate Casey for longer. He wished Natalie was here now.

"Then I met Lauren," Morgan said, moving her finger around the rim of her coffee cup. "I told her our story. She googled you one night. We were drunk. She was making fun of your tie."

Scott smiled, thinking of Lauren being so silly. "My tie?"

"You had to be there. Lauren's always made me laugh." Morgan stared down, lower lip trembling. "She was looking for a job as a teaching assistant, and since we were on your school's faculty page, job listings were right there. That's how she found out about it. She said she could maybe get close to you, learn a little about what happened to Natalie."

"Jesus," Scott whispered, thinking of the dog.

It was so silly; as the hours turned to two days, Scott tried to label it as a pain-induced hallucination, nothing more. But it had felt so real. And it was the same with this; there was no man, surely, to whom the phrase *God's plan* was more appropriate.

Idiot. He pushed it all away, focused.

"You know what happened to Natalie," Gary snapped. "What are you trying to imply?"

Morgan sat up straight. "She killed herself the night she was going to leave Scott. We had planned it for months. She was

244

going to move in with me, then we were going to tell her parents. She was so nervous about it. She kept putting it off, putting it off, until I gave her an ultimatum. She'd give me a date, or I'd leave her."

Morgan shuddered. "I shouldn't have said that. Natalie could get anxious, volatile. I was so angry, I scratched out my name. I even gave Natalie's bracelet to Lauren."

Scott nodded; he knew too well how unpredictable his wife could be. She'd been good in so many ways. They'd shared so much love and laughter. Scott noticed Gary shaking his head, as though this version of Natalie didn't make sense. Scott wondered if that's why Lauren was always fiddling with the bracelet, as a bizarre connection to his dead wife.

"I asked her to quit almost straightaway," Morgan went on. "It was too weird. You weren't going to tell her anything. And even if you had anything to tell, I'm not sure I'd want to know. Natalie took her life because of me."

"Or I killed her." Scott laughed grimly. "That's what you and Lauren were thinking."

"I didn't rule it out."

"I'd never hurt Natalie."

"Lauren likes you, Scott. She thinks you're a good person. Even after I asked her to quit, she kept working with you. She said you were a good teacher, a role model to the children. But look where it got her. She may never wake up. And all because of your wife."

Scott didn't have the energy to fight. He felt hollow after everything that had happened. "I know."

Morgan bit down on her fingernail. "I guess we'll wait."

"Yeah," Scott said. "I guess we will."

53

SCOTT

"Lauren's awake," Morgan said over the phone, six days after they met in the hospital.

Scott was sitting in the garden, trying to focus on a novel; even before the phone call, he hadn't been able to concentrate.

Now he smiled. He sat up. He felt *not numb*.

"Oh, thank God," he said, and he meant it. He couldn't stop thinking about that dog. "Can I speak to her?"

"When she's ready," Morgan said. "She's still very tired. And there may be complications. Brain damage. We don't know yet."

"Morgan, I'm so sorry."

"Me too, Scott," she replied. "For everything. And... and thank you for sharing Natalie's note with me."

He'd given it to her the day before, when they'd met at the hospital; things were never great between Morgan, Gary and Scott, but they were civil. And they all had a common goal in mind: for Lauren to wake up, for her to be okay.

"I don't think I said thanks," Morgan said.

"Did it help?"

She sighed. "I hope it helped her. Thinking of me. But I've got to focus on Lauren now."

They said goodbye, and Scott wondered if he should tell Morgan the truth. But then, it wasn't *the* truth; it was his experience with her.

Scott grinned; he was getting messed up. And right then, he paused, really feeling the grin.

The afternoon sun on his face. He closed his eyes and saw the dog.

I don't have to be who you want me to be, he thought, in *his* voice, and he was talking to Natalie. *I can be my own man. I'm sorry. I don't want to be with you anymore.*

The next day, he decided to do something about the mess. He was limited to how much he could do, considering his busted ankle and his crutches. But he'd try.

Listening to Christian music – he'd laughed at himself as he selected the playlist, but he selected it anyway – he did his best. He folded cardboard boxes and packed them for recycling as he leaned against the counter. He rubbed down the surfaces; he collected all the dishes and put them in the washer.

Ah, he needed dishwasher tabs.

He walked awkwardly to the undercounter cupboard where they kept all their bits and bobs: carrier bags and dishwasher tablets and cleaning supplies of every kind. This had been Casey's domain while they were married; he still caught himself thinking of her sometimes, smiling at him across the kitchen.

Leaning down, he winced, reaching to the back of the cupboard; he couldn't find the bloody things...

His hand brushed something. It felt like paper. And there was duct tape.

Just like with the notebook.

Scott felt around, to the end of the tape, pulled softly; he felt the paper coming away.

He was breathing hard.

Taking the note out, he read it; he read it all several times, then he began to laugh. So hard his chest hurt. So hard he crumpled in a ball on the kitchen floor, lying on his side, trembling with the laughter; tears streamed sideways down his face and his ankle cast bumped against the floor, and he kept on.

All for her fucking writing class, he thought, and laughed even harder. *Jesus bloody Christ.*

And yet he lingered on the end too, the part where she'd said she was sorry.

The laughter broke up. He sucked in drowning sobs.

And even now, he wished she was here.

54

NATALIE

gain I return to these short passages; I'm often jealous of the Natalie who was able to write this: what amounts to a couple of dozen paltry pages. It's so pathetic, really, how proud I am of this story, this writing exercise. I never even showed it to the teacher. I don't think I'm going to.

It was like she said, experimental method writing, branding my character with my husband's name. "I *love* that idea; it will make it so much more visceral and shocking to you, and so it will to the reader. Do it."

I did it, but now I read them again, and I feel rotten. I'm not sure what sickness is inside of me.

What the fuck am I doing? It's like a fractured mirror; it's like the mirror is in my eyes and reality is upside down. I don't know. I can't think anymore. I can't focus. I just wish it would stop.

It. *Me*. Everything.

I'm going to burn this, I think, all of it. I can't tell anybody, but I can't keep it in either.

I have not been a good wife to Scott. I hit him.

Not once; I *have* hit him, I *do* hit him.

I don't mean to, but sometimes my rage just flashes, and it happens. Before I know it, I'm slapping my hand across his face, screaming. I once scratched him so badly he thought he was going to lose his sight. I didn't mean to; I was aiming for his cheek, but anger made me clumsy.

Every time, he holds me. He tells me he's sorry for whatever provoked it; once, he told me he'd try his best not to make me angry in the future.

I need to get control of my anger. But sometimes it's like I can trick myself into believing it's all his fault. *He's* the one standing between me and Morgan, even if I know that's ridiculous.

If I can't leave him, and if I can't stop letting my anger become physical, I know what I'll do. I've rehearsed it a few times now, in case life ever becomes too difficult.

I'll go through with my plan, and then Morgan can move on, find someone else, someone… *not me.* Scott will be better for it, after he mourns me; he loves me so deeply, so loyally.

Maybe it'll be easier after, when it's up to God to decide.

I'm back. I still hate myself. I can't believe I wrote this. But of course I did. I'm nothing but filth.

It would be easier to slit my throat than say I'm sorry.

I really do love him.

Again, I'm here, looking over my work: that warped world where I made Scott the villain. It was good to immerse myself in the fever dream of this other Scott. He's the one who did all those terrible things; he deserves it every time, as though my most intense moments of anger become my entire judgement of him.

It's how I felt, writing those passages; often I was in, I don't know what you'd call it, a frenzy. I couldn't stop and I was so amped-up, wanting to believe it.

There's nothing normal in this life I've lived, the choices I've made.

But I do love him. That's the hardest part. It's just like there's this switch, and he hits it, and I just *flood* with... And that's the worst thought, the one which comes naturally, birthed from childhood. With Satan, with the devil, Lucifer whelming inside my soul, until there's nothing else left.

I don't believe it, not intellectually, not emotionally. Not physically or anything else. But there's an ebb there, down deep, as though at the root of me. I can't ever cut it away.

But my enemy – everybody's enemy – is said to prowl like a lion looking for something to devour. That's... Peter, maybe. Is it prowling inside me, waiting for a chance to come out?

Morgan and I did nothing wrong. Apart from the affair.

But our love mattered. Perhaps I will tell Mum and Dad.

Or maybe I'll just go through with my plan.

I can't keep doing this. Hurting him. Hating myself for it, and hating him more for letting it happen.

I wish I could tell him I was sorry. And mean it. And not snap again.

I wish the tears after every fight could stay with me. But they always fade. And even if I'm thinking – *I promised I wouldn't do this* – I can't stop the hate. Not in the moment. Not right then.

I just fucking *hate*.

I hate life.

I don't want to be here.

That's it. I think that's really it.

I've made up my mind.

If I don't burn this, Scott, just know I'm sorry. I really, truly am so sorry for what I've done to us.

55

SCOTT

ONE YEAR LATER

"I think my religious journey really started with my mother."

Scott stood at the front of Gary's living room; his friend, although not agreeing with Scott's new religious streak, was still there for him. When Scott had told him he was getting baptised, Gary had smiled tightly. He'd all but said he could never believe what Scott did.

And yet Gary had offered to throw the party. Scott smiled over at him, where he sat with Aissa. Joseph, a friend from church, sat next to him. Lauren and Morgan were in the corner, and all around there were more people, the atmosphere warm.

Colleagues from school. Scott's mother in the corner, smiling encouragingly; she'd been so happy when he gave her the news. At church, during the ceremony itself, he'd heard her weeping gently as the water rushed over his head.

Everybody agreed, despite their personal views, it was good for Scott. His religion had helped him deal with the aftermath of the abuse: *both* periods, with Casey, yes... but also with Natalie. With her rages, with her violence, her crying, her saying sorry.

"I lost my way, and it led me into some bad places. But the

truth is, God saved me that night. He came to me and he gave me the strength to act. He saved me, and I think he saved you too, Lauren."

Lauren looked around, grinning ironically. Scott was so glad the injuries hadn't had any lasting effect. She was still her usual cutting self; she'd quit school and was training to become a police officer. She was doing great.

"Oh yeah," she said. "*God* saved me. It was you, Scott."

A few of his church friends turned their noses up at that, but he never would.

"The point is," he went on, "whatever a person believes–"

Several phones went off at the same time; Scott's buzzed from his pocket. Gary's made a notification sound from the arm of the chair. Even his mum's.

Everybody looked around, laughing awkwardly.

"That's weird," somebody said, but Scott couldn't hear them; it was all crashing down.

Gary stared at him, and he knew. He saw it coming.

All that faith he'd put into God's plan, into thinking He'd taken him through this to lead him to Him. And now people were checking their phones; Gary's hand rushed for his. Aissa could tell something was wrong; she was clutching Gary's arm, looking back and forth.

Scott took dreamlike steps backwards, feeling like he could fall off the edge.

Any edge.

Casey hadn't known the emails of his church friends; *he* hadn't known them then. But Joseph leaned over and looked at Gary's phone.

Everybody would see.

"Oh, Scott." Gary stood, strode over. "Jesus. I'm so... fuck, Scott."

"Did she write a message, or was it just the files?"

Gary showed him his phone.

If you killed me, Scottie darling, see you soon. I'll keep your bed nice and warm for you. If I'm in prison, well... I'm a patient woman. Lots of love, your doting wife, Casey xxx

No, she was alive, in a psychiatric prison. Scott hoped they never let her out.

Scott took Gary's phone, clicked the first attachment.

The first minute was a slideshow of photos: all of which had clearly been taken in secret.

THE END

ACKNOWLEDGEMENTS

I would like to thank everybody on the Bloodhound Books team who helped bring this novel to life. In particular: Betsy Reavley and the submissions team for taking a chance on my fairly 'different' books; Fred Freeman for his tireless work in trying to make us as successful as possible; Tara Lyons for her attention to detail and positivity; Hannah Deuce for always making sure our books shine on social media; and Morgen Bailey, my editor, whose insight is always valuable and who has saved my books more than once.

As for people outside the bookish world, in the past I have named specific friends and family members etc., but the truth is, there are far too many people to thank. A writer's job is a unique one. Our blessing is that everybody, everywhere, is interesting to us; there are few activities or situations a writer won't find fascinating in some way, if only for possible inspiration. Maybe that's why I've been blessed with friends who range from rollerblading lunatics to intellectual and bookish types. I feel incredibly fortunate in this regard.

To all my friends, my family, I say thank you from the bottom of my heart.

However, there is one person I will always mention by name. Without Krystle, my wife, I am fully convinced I never would've become a writer. Our marriage stands in stark contrast to the types of people I write about; it's only through knowing how good and constructive marriage can be, I feel I'm able to flip it and study the evil side. So the final thank you goes to

Krystle, without whom I'd probably be still trying to find my way, lost in life, wondering where I'm going; it's impossible to overstate how integral her support has been in my writing career.

Finally, I'd like to thank the most important person: yes, that's right, even more so than Krystle (she never reads my acknowledgements pages). *You*, the reader; I'm so grateful that you decided to take a chance on this book, and I hope you stick around for the next one.

A NOTE FROM THE PUBLISHER

Thank you for reading this book. If you enjoyed it please do consider leaving a review on Amazon to help others find it too.

We hate typos. All of our books have been rigorously edited and proofread, but sometimes mistakes do slip through. If you have spotted a typo, please do let us know and we can get it amended within hours.

info@bloodhoundbooks.com

Printed in Great Britain
by Amazon